THE POCKET UNIVERSE

R. Bruce Sundrud

Chapter One

Madison heard Nanny Bee's footsteps but tried to ignore them, to stay in her pleasant dream. She was floating peacefully. Why did Nanny have to break into her sleep?

She heard Nanny spread wide the bedroom curtains, letting in the early morning sunshine. It was spring, and dawn came early, way too early. Her bedroom window was on the second floor of the tavern, and because her window faced east, the sun's rays flowed into her room and through her eyelids, pulling her completely awake.

"Ack!" She plummeted onto her bed. "Nanny!"

"Yes, dear?"

"Do you have to do that every morning? Can't you just let me sleep in for once?"

"The early bird gets the worm, dear."

"I know, you've said that a thousand times." She pushed her hair back from her face. "And the poor worm gets punished for rising early. He should have slept in."

"And you've answered that way a thousand times, and it wasn't original the first time. You've got to get more creative, young lady. I should talk to Uncle Roddyn about having you study more poetry." Nanny Bee, wearing sensible black shoes and a pinafore apron over her blue work dress, pulled the pillows out from under Madison's head and began fluffing them.

"Don't talk to Uncle Roddyn!" Madison slid out of bed and into her fleece-lined slippers. "He'll make me read some bizarre stuff from Japan or India." She rubbed her eyes and walked to the window. Nanny Bee kept the windows sparkling clean all year round, and Madison had to shield her eyes from the sun so that she could look out onto the lawn.

The back yard of the tavern called The Padded Cell stretched all the way to the foothills and took in an orchard of fruit trees and an excellent fishing stream left untouched from the pioneer days. Some of the early trees were blossoming and the cherry trees, her favorites, were covered with pale pink flowers. She lifted the window, hoping to smell some fragrance, but could only inhale the mustiness of waking earth.

Something was walking between the cherry trees.

Madison watched carefully, instantly alert. Whatever it was, it gave a little hop and she saw a shower of sparks. A branch suddenly shed its blossoms and became heavy with dark red cherries.

"Uh-oh. Something Escaped." Madison kicked off her slippers and pulled her nightgown over her head.

"Shouldn't you call your uncle?"

Madison pulled on her work jeans and snapped them up. "It's nothing big. I don't need Uncle Roddyn." She slipped on a t-shirt that said I'm Not Indecisive…Right? and pushed her feet into a pair of worn sneakers.

Time to order new shoes, now that spring is here. I wish I could outgrow a pair just once instead of wearing them out.

She checked her hair in the mirror on her way out. It was a mess, as usual. It was brown and naturally curly and when she slept on it, it always got into tangles before she could relax and elevate above the bed. She was fourteen, but she was still skinny and her figure hadn't started developing. She had tried eating

3

larger portions over winter, hoping the extra weight would help, but her rapid metabolism betrayed her.

She sighed and ruffed up her hair, making it worse. Then she opened her bedroom door and took the carpeted stairs two steps at a time, landing as quietly as she could. No one came into the tavern this early, and the tiny kitchen only served lunch and dinner. Uncle Roddyn, the Caretaker, usually slept in, having kept the bar open the night before.

She crossed the polished wooden floor and passed the booth where Emtianal lived, but he was also asleep, his avatar leaning against the side of the booth, its eyes shut.

The back door exited beside the kitchen and the hated trash cans. Her daily chore was to haul the tavern's full cans out to the highway, a two hundred yard trek. She used a large wagon to haul the cans but the yard was uneven and there was always the danger of tipping, and then oh! what a horrid mess to clean.

She hurried across the lawn, ignoring the cold dew that soaked her sneakers. She rubbed her fingers together and sparks twinkled on her fingertips as magic concentrated in them.

What is that thing?

The Escaped creature stood about shoulder-high to her, but that included the peaked hat shaped like a dunce cap. It wore a purple robe covered with strange symbols, and the hat had stylized stars all over it.

It had a muzzle, so it wasn't human, but it ran on two legs and gestured with two arms like a little child. In one hand it held a staff that ended in a large gem. As Madison watched, it waved the staff at a branch and cried, *"Umleet a shivekka!"*

The branch lost its blossoms, and golden apricots appeared. The creature hopped and clapped its paws. *"Hee hee heee!"*

The Escaped so reminded Madison of a rat that she labeled it the Rat Witch. "Speak the Common Tongue," she commanded, and flicked her fingers at it.

The Rat Witch whirled and ducked, and the spell flew harmlessly over her head. She glared at Madison with large black eyes. *"Eeya mooglit!"* she snarled, shaking a fist.

Madison resented being called a *mooglit*, whatever that was. Before she could ready another spell, the Rat Witch reached into her robe and pulled out a small black ball. She flung it at Madison and the ball burst into flame in midair.

Madison caught it smartly and juggled it like a hot potato, keeping an insulating layer of magic on her hands. The ball felt like pumice and smelled of sulfur.

Nasty little creature.

She threw the fireball back at the Rat Witch and while the creature was dodging, she cast her spell again. "Speak the Common Tongue!"

This spell flew faster and brighter and struck the Rat Witch head-on. She cried, "Woop!" and flipped over on her back.

Madison walked up slowly, not trusting the creature, but she seemed to be out cold. Her face was a cross between a rat and a spiteful little girl with skin problems. The staff was made of a rich dark wood, topped off by a green gem, probably an emerald, held in place with strips of leather.

She placed the staff on the Rat Witch's chest and scooped her up with both arms. "Time for you to go back," she muttered, and carried her across the lawn towards the door to the wine cellar.

Before she reached it, the back door opened and Uncle Roddyn stepped out. His long gray hair was pulled back into a pony tail; he had serious-looking eyebrows over his dark eyes and a gray walrus mustache under his veined nose. He looked as though whoever had put him together had used too much material in his shoulders and had too little left over for the hands. They were strong hands, though, able to crush the juice out of a lemon without a squeezer. He was barefoot, a sign that he had just thrown on some clothes before coming outside. "You found something?"

"Did Nanny wake you up?"

"Maddy, you're going to get in trouble one of these days. Something might get out that you can't handle. You should have called me."

"Well, this one was like, nothing. My Common Tongue spell knocked her flat." She may be only fourteen, but she wasn't helpless.

"That doesn't mean that the next thing that wanders out won't eat you alive and spit out the pieces, so call me, darn it, the next time you see something running loose." He put his hand on the carved wooden letters that said WINE CELLAR and pushed them to the side. He waited for the rumble from the slanted cellar door to finish, and then grabbed the handle and lifted it open. A bright glow from the cellar lit his face. "Here, give me that." He took the Rat Witch with one arm, and the staff with the other. He frowned and looked at the staff closely.

The Rat Witch suddenly awoke and cried out, grasping for the staff.

"Oh, no, you don't," said Uncle Roddyn. He laid the staff on the top steps, and carried her down into the cellar.

"My staff! Gives me back my staff!" the Rat Witch wailed, but her cries were cut off and Uncle Roddyn walked back up the steps empty handed. "That's that." He picked up the staff and looked at it from all sides. "I need to study this."

He put the cellar door down with his free hand and pushed the WINE CELLAR plaque back into place. The cellar rumbled again.

"She's back in her own world?"

"Yes, it was still there at the surface, but she wasn't happy about it." He tucked the staff under his arm. "Now, don't you have some cans to haul?"

"Yes, sir," she said, grimacing. She always did her chores, but never happily. Anything was better than hauling garbage cans, even studying Emily Dickinson, who couldn't keep a straight thought or finish a sentence. She smacked her forehead. "And it's Wednesday. Oh, spit!"

6

The sooner the better.

She tied her sneakers properly, and then got the large rusty wagon from the shed. It used to be bright red, but the years had worn it down. One wheel wobbled and squeaked, but bravely rolled on.

She put two of the garbage cans from the kitchen into the wagon, trying hard not to breathe in the smell of yesterday's food, and grabbed the handle. She let a little magic slide into the wagon, and it pulled easily, even over the grass.

There were twenty yards of grass between The Padded Cell's front doors and the asphalt parking lot, and new customers complained about the walk. "You need to make some closer spaces for the handicapped," they would say, and Uncle Roddyn would nod and continue mixing drinks. "No more for me," another would say, "I've got to walk all the way back to my car." "No one ever drives away drunk," said another, "They walk it off before they get behind the wheel."

By the time she got to the parking lot her magic had diminished, as always happened when she got away from the tavern, and the wagon got harder to pull. Fortunately, the driveway was paved out to the highway where the daily garbage truck came by. She left the two cans there and returned for the other kitchen garbage can and the recyclable containers. Having recyclables to put out was new, and the county only sent their truck around on Wednesdays, and since this was Wednesday, she had lots of containers full of empty bottles and cans to haul. It took her three trips.

Finally she was done and able to shower and shampoo her hair. The new crème rinse that Mrs. Regan had brought her from Sharonville seemed to tame some of the wild fluffiness, and the tangles seemed more subdued as she combed them out. Electricity didn't work well in The Padded Cell, so she couldn't use a blow dryer. Electric lights worked, but electric motors wore out quickly and gas motors were hard to start. In an hour her hair would be dry and she could brush it into a semblance of order.

She stared at her face, as she did every morning. She wanted more cheekbones and less cheek. She wanted a smaller nose and darker eyebrows and brown or blue eyes, not the storm-flecked gray that changed color with her surroundings. She wanted earlobes that would stay pierced and not close up overnight.

She also wanted a figure and, oh, why not, a million dollars to go with it. Make that two million.

Nanny Bee had made Madison's bed and lined everything up picture-perfect, slippers and all. Madison tossed her jeans in the direction of the hamper – garbage jeans got smelly fast – threw her T-shirt in the direction of the closet, and pulled on some khakis and a fresh T-shirt that said Everyone Hates Me Because I'm Paranoid. She clipped a charm bracelet around her neck – circus animals – and popped a stick of watermelon bubble gum into her mouth.

She was ready to face another day.

Chapter Two

Madison worked in the kitchen from ten in the morning until two in the afternoon every day except Sunday, slapping together sandwiches and preparing The Padded Cell's soup of the day. She no longer needed a recipe for the soup pot; she knew ten different soup recipes and for each recipe she knew just how many shakes of the pepper shaker was needed, what size palmful of salt, and exactly how many pinches of other spices would add just the right bouquet. By eleven the soup would be ready, and anyone ordering soup after the lunch hour would be lucky to get some. On Saturdays she made a double batch – this Saturday she planned on broccoli and cheese – and Sundays they were closed.

A hired cook came at two o'clock and worked the kitchen until it closed at ten. The current cook was a woman with hairy arms, cold eyes and no humor, so Madison stayed out of her way. The cook complained about not having a mixer and a fan, but the dinner menu was basically fried things and the gas stove worked just fine.

Pinhead helped with what he could, of course. Madison knew how to guide Pinhead so that he was useful, but the cook didn't want to bother – she said he was spooky – so for the rest of the day Uncle Roddyn had him tending the landscape in summer or shoveling snow or cutting logs in the winter. Pinhead was an Escaped, but harmless and about as sharp as a billiard ball. He reminded Madison of a small egg, balanced on a large egg.

"Isn't that a little mean, calling him Pinhead?" a customer once asked, but Madison explained that Pinhead didn't have any other name. The customer frowned and didn't return.

Madison didn't get a paycheck – she was too young and there were laws. When she was working, the regulars would be sure to holler "Hi, Sheriff!" when Sheriff Carson stopped in. She would quietly drop her apron and go sit at Emtianal's booth and deal out some cards. Carson would say hi to her in passing, and then go sit by the window and have his coffee and bear claw – on the house – while he surveyed the cars in the parking lot.

Before she started kitchen work, though, she had to study and do her chores. The garbage had to be at the curbside by 7:30 in the morning, and then she was expected to be washed, dressed, and seated at a dining table by a quarter after eight, hitting her books. Early American authors and geology were the topics this month; geology was interesting but Dickinson drove her mad.

> Though the great Waters sleep,
> That they are still the Deep,
> We cannot doubt –
> No vacillating God
> Ignited this Abode
> To put it out –

"Sentences are supposed to end in PERIODS not DASHES, you ninny!" she growled at her book of collected poems.

"Huh?" said Pinhead, passing by with an armload of firewood.

"Nothing. I wasn't yelling at you. Good morning!" She smiled at him and he smiled back vacantly. He lumbered on to the fireplace.

The ancient stone hearth of The Padded Cell was the pride of the tavern. Large enough that two men could sleep inside it – not that any ever did – the iron grate held logs cut longer than

10

usual. It cast a lovely heat into the tavern and dining area during the winters. With spring arriving, this might be the last time that Pinhead made a fire.

The foothills were densely wooded with oak and poplar, and Pinhead walked out each day even in the worst of snows to chop logs for the hearth. Madison had asked if Pinhead could be taught to haul the garbage cans also, but Uncle Roddyn said that he looked too "startling" to be out by the highway. Besides, it was character-building for Madison to haul garbage.

Right.

Scratched into the concrete on the side of the hearth was a date: 1824. "The tavern's older than that," Uncle Roddyn said, "but the rest of it has been rebuilt." Even Madison's bedroom had new double-pane windows to keep it comfortable summer or winter, though they were of a style that matched the tavern's historic appearance.

She sighed and looked at a few other poems by Dickinson. They were better constructed – in later years Emily D. seemed to have rediscovered the period at the end of sentences – and Madison tried to pull some meaning out of them. She wrote some notes on the poems for Sunday afternoon's Grand Homework Review by Uncle Roddyn, and poked through her geology text.

Volcanoes fascinated her, the way that they had built up the Hawaiian Islands over time, and the destruction at Pompeii. Even Mount Majestic to the north of the tavern was an extinct volcano, featured on local postcards. Madison felt that it was brooding and mysterious rather than scenic, and she was disappointed that it had not blown up.

She had never been to Mount Majestic. She had never been to Sharonville. She got uneasy when she got any distance from the tavern, and her magic ceased to work. Further than that and she felt downright ill. She could walk out to the highway or up the fishing stream to the first falls, and that was it.

Her books were brought from the Sharonville Public Library by Mrs. Regan, a widow who felt it her duty in life to help others, which included bringing a monthly set of serious books for Madison to study, plus some novels for entertainment. Madison preferred mysteries and historical fiction, and anything Stephen King would crank out. Vampire novels, on the other hand, made her nervous. They seemed too real.

The new crème rinse was an attempt by Mrs. Regan to tame Madison's wild brown hair.

Madison wrote down the definitions of horst and graben – a *horst* was a raised section of land due to geologic faults, and a *graben* was a valley for the same reason – and tucked her notebook into the storage room shelf next to the dozens of other notebooks she had filled over the years. She laid the book of Emily Dickinson's Greatest Works on the shelf next to it, and covered the book with the geology text as though she were hiding dirt under a rug.

They had no internet – the electricity thing again – or TV. Madison was sure that she was missing something terribly fascinating and important, but the customers didn't mind the lack of televisions all over the walls. It was part of the unique charm of The Padded Cell. People actually talked to each other, or watched the logs burn, or played cards with Emtianal, or on festive occasions brought instruments and played while others sang and danced.

"Where did the name, The Padded Cell, come from?" people would ask Roddyn as he worked behind the bar.

"Country records say this tavern used to be called Tom O'Bedlam," he stroked his mustache thoughtfully, "but people kept thinking that it was a private residence of some Irish family. The last owners changed the name to The Padded Cell. Considering some of our customers, I think it's appropriate." He would wink at them, and they would smile back. They knew that everyone else was crazy but them.

"Horst and graben," Madison repeated as she walked to the kitchen and grabbed a clean white apron. She slipped her head through the upper loop and tied the strings behind her. Then she covered her unruly hair with a hair net and said to herself, "I be 'graben' a fast 'horst' from the stable." She laughed at her own puns – no one else would – and pulled a vegetable knife from the drawer. As she sharpened it with a stone, Pinhead stepped in.

"Can I help?" he asked, rocking slowly side to side.

"Sure. You can dice the potatoes for me." She pulled a ten-pound sack of potatoes from a storage bin and set it on the chopping block with a knife beside it.

Pinhead stared at the potatoes and put a finger in his mouth. "What do I do?"

Madison began twisting stalks from a head of celery. "Put on an apron."

"Okay." Pinhead turned slowly until he saw the clean aprons hanging by the back door. He put his head through a loop, and backed up to Madison so she could tie it. He turned around, and his eyes brightened. "Oh! Dice potatoes!" He put on a hair net even though he only had a small curly knot of hair on the top of his head, scrubbed his hands, picked up the knife, slit open the bag, and began rinsing the potatoes.

Without the apron, Pinhead had no clue what to do about potatoes. With the apron, he diced the potatoes perfectly every time, no cut fingers, no mess. It was the same way with chopping logs for the fire; unless he put on his woodman's hat as he picked up the axe, he was helpless. With the hat on, he treated the forest with wisdom and care.

Today, the Padded Cell's Soup of the Day was going to be vegetable beef, which included diced potatoes with the peel left on; it always had, and it always would; no one complained. Celery, sun-dried tomatoes, barley, beef, carrots, cabbage, herbs and spices all simmered in the pot for an hour, and then it was served up and gone. Madison always reserved a cup for Uncle Roddyn before it ran out, and Pinhead swallowed two. When people asked for the recipe, Uncle Roddyn shrugged. "There isn't one. It's all in Maddy's head."

The regular cook never made soup for her shift. If anyone asked for soup, she just grunted, "Not my job."

Madison finished serving lunch, helped Pinhead remove his apron, and went to her room to wash up. It was warm and sunny, so she changed into knee-length shorts and yet another t-shirt, a frayed one that read "Pillage, THEN burn." She took the stairs three at a time – not easy – and charged out the back door towards the maintenance shed at the edge of the orchard.

The shed not only housed the push lawn mower – Pinhead's summer job – and other equipment, it had an ice maker, a water heater, and a washer and dryer, being far enough away from the tavern that electric motors worked well. Nanny Bee was watching the washer sloshing away at a load of laundry. Madison recruited her for some Frisbee tossing.

Madison ran back and forth, catching the plastic disc behind her back, popping it up into the air with her fingertips, and trying to throw it under her leg. Nanny patiently walked to the disc when it inevitably went astray, and fired it back towards Madison with absolute accuracy. Only stray breezes could send it askew when Nanny threw it, so Madison would often ask Nanny to throw it to either side so that she would have to run for it.

She worked up a sweat and stopped to glug some water from a hose. The water came from a natural spring above the first falls, clean and cold.

"I need to fold," said Nanny Bee, and Madison tossed the plastic disc into the shed and ran back to the tavern. No one needed to help Nanny; she was tireless.

Madison toweled down and changed yet again. Knowing she might run into Mrs. Regan, she put on long pants and a red t-shirt with "I think, therefore we have nothing in common" emblazoned on it. It was a new t-shirt, another gift from Mrs. Regan. It was also her fourth t-shirt of the day, but it made her feel fresh. Nanny Bee did laundry often.

Madison grabbed her current Agatha Christie novel and went down to a rocker on the front porch to see how Hercule

Poirot was dealing with the many-stabbed body on the Orient Express. She rested the book in her lap and looked out at the driveway beyond the parking lot.

The tavern had a small sign at the end of the driveway, indicating that the establishment was "The Padded Cell, Tavern and Diner." The sign was lit until midnight, but the regulars often didn't leave until one. Uncle Roddyn didn't believe in any other advertising. Quiet times and a small but loyal clientele were fine for him. The tavern had no mortgage, and they had little to spend their earnings on.

One by one the customers dropped in. "Hi, Maddy," said a black machinist with clean but patched overalls, on his way to the night shift in Waterton.

Maddy waved, keeping her eyes on the printed words.

How could every single person on the train car be a suspect?

"Hey, Maddy."

She lifted her hand at the retired postal worker with gray hair and a rumpled sweater.

"Nose in a book again, eh?" This was Sheryl, plain but friendly. She was secretary to a Realtor in Sharonville and was always good for a game of cards with Emtianal after she had eaten.

Madison looked up and smiled, holding the book so Sheryl could see the title.

Sheryl pursed her lips. "Oh, that one. I couldn't believe it was the conductor that killed the..."

"No! Don't tell!" Madison cupped her hands over her ears and began singing loudly.

Sheryl laughed. "Just kidding. I never got to the end. Too English for me."

"Can we do cards after you eat?"

"Sure. I'll poke my head out and call you."

Maddy nodded and returned to her book.

Emtianal's avatar was awake and smiling, and his hands moved with dexterity as he shuffled and dealt. Rummy was their game, although Madison had tried to get him to teach her how to play poker.

"No," he whispered. "It is gambling, and you are underage."

Underage.

I'm fourteen and I've been fourteen forever. And when I finally get to fifteen, I'll still be underage.

Life was so unfair.

She had watched poker games from the top of the stairs when she should have been sleeping. Emtianal played below his capacity during poker games, being careful to lose as much as he won. He could have made big money, but it would have been bad for the tavern and bad for him. As a result, nobody paid much attention to him during a game. He never got out of his booth to stretch or to use the restrooms.

Ever.

Uncle Roddyn set a mug of lemonade beside Madison and a glass of milk with a straw in front of Emtianal. Sheryl nursed her Derby Special, heavy on the lime. Roddyn asked, "Mind if I play? Things are slow right now."

Sheryl nodded, and Madison said, "Sure."

"A shame this is not for money," whispered Emtianal, gathering the cards and dealing them out again. "I would enjoy winning this tavern from you." His avatar had wavy brown hair on his handsome head, with large dark eyes and a wide mouth. His delicate fingers could do wonders with cards, but he had long ago assured Madison that he was scrupulously honest when it came to Rummy.

"Just deal," said Roddyn, his mouth serious under his thick mustache.

Emtianal was very life-like when Sheryl and the other customers were around. Madison could see a sheen of magic on

16

him then, very delicate.   His expressions were animated, he laughed, his eyes crinkled, and his voice was strong.

When Madison played cards with him all by herself, his expression did not change, win or lose, and sometimes when he was studying his cards he angled them towards his face as though looking at them through his mouth.

He sipped his milk after dealing – Sheryl was there so he was careful to close his lips around the straw before sucking it up – and flipped the top card to start a discard pile.   Then he laid down a run of four hearts, nine through queen, and drew a fresh card.

Sheryl added a king of hearts on Emtianal's run and drew her card to end her turn. "Lucky so-and-so," she muttered.

Roddyn drew a card and frowned at it, then dropped a two of clubs on the discard pile.

"Isn't Friday night the vernal equinox?" Emtianal asked as Madison pondered her hand.

"Uh-huh," said Roddyn, rearranging his cards.

"Is the Jug and Fiddle band going to play here again?"

"Uh-huh. As usual."

Madison discarded a two of hearts and drew a fresh card. She could really use a joker. Nothing in her hand seemed to mesh.

The Vernal Equinox.   That's the day I bake myself a birthday cake.

"That's good," Emtianal whispered. "I enjoy a live band."

"Barely a live band, considering their age," said Roddyn. "If the regulars didn't clap and holler, they'd probably fall asleep."

"But they are enjoyable," said Emtianal. "Don't they play anywhere else?"

"I don't think so. The only songs they know are Golden Oldies, anyway. Are you going to play or what?"

Emtianal dropped an eight of hearts on his own run, and discarded a three of diamonds. "Don't other places celebrate the equinox?"

Roddyn shook his head, making his mustache shake. "We're old-fashioned that way, so there's no competition. On the other hand, we're almost empty on New Year's Eve. Everyone else has a band, and they all want to be up at Sharonville to watch the giant wrench drop at midnight."

"Whoopee," said Madison without enthusiasm.

Sheryl laid down three fives and drew a fresh card.

But if I could travel, I would be there.

If I could travel, I would be at Times Square.

Roddyn and Madison each drew a card and discarded.

Still no joker.

Emtianal drew a card, laid down a five on Sheryl's three fives, dropped an ace of hearts on his own run, and finished with the required discard. "Rummy," he announced, spreading his empty hands.

"Ah, crud!" Roddyn dropped his hand on the table. He had gotten caught with face cards and two aces for a big penalty.

Madison scored the round – she was always the scorekeeper, Roddyn said, because it was part of her education – and Sheryl shuffled. As she finished dealing out the cards, a couple of motorcycles pulled up to the front door, big road bikes by their throaty rumble.

"Why can't they keep those things in the parking lot instead on the sidewalk? Now I bet they won't start up again. Pardon me," Roddyn said, going to the bar. Sheryl gathered the cards and dealt again for just the three of them.

A couple of regulars in their late thirties walked in. The man, Mitch Mackenzie, pulled off a leather aviator's cap and hung it on one of the wooden pegs by the door. He had studs in his ears and the back of his leather jacket sported a Harley logo with flames, and he hollered loudly for a couple of beers. The woman, Penny Rusting – she joked with Madison about the name – had heavily colored, stiff-sprayed red hair and a tattoo of an eagle on her forearm. She was a strong woman, but she usually let Mitch do the talking. Both wore heavy jeans and ornate black leather belts. They ran a combination antique and bikers' shop on the

18

outskirts of the state capitol, but closed it often to tour the state on their Harley-Davidson Electra Glides.

In spite of their rough appearance, they were a friendly couple. Uncle Roddyn chatted with them about the Vernal equinox party coming up – Madison remembered that Mitch and Penny had helped her Uncle tend bar at the Fall equinox event – the lovely spring weather and what a good day it was to ride, and weren't the county commissioners a bunch of – she couldn't overhear the term – for closing the railroad overpass to Gunderson?

Emtianal played conservatively this round and Sheryl was ahead in points when Nanny Bee stepped in through the back door. She gestured to Madison.

"Excuse me," said Madison, and she scooted back her chair and walked to Nanny Bee. "What is it?"

"I don't mean to disturb you," said Nanny in a low voice, "but Mr. Roddyn is busy." She pointed out the back door. "There is a ghost standing under the oak tree and he says that he would like to talk with someone."

Chapter Three

Madison touched Sheryl on the shoulder. "Nanny needs me to help her outside. Sorry."

Sheryl smiled and dropped her cards onto the table. "Go on, then. Maybe tomorrow we'll start over."

"That would be fine," whispered Emtianal, gathering the cards together. "Anytime."

Madison hurried out the back door.

A ghost under the oak tree?

The highway ran north of the tavern, and beyond that towered Mount Majestic. The orchard and fishing stream lay to the south. Off the tavern's west corner, a hundred yards towards the setting sun, stood a massive oak tree. Madison could not reach its lowest branches and so usually left it alone. There was much better climbing in the orchard, and sometimes fruit.

She followed Nanny to the old oak tree and sure enough, there stood a man, but he was difficult to see.

Clouds obscured the setting sun, but that was not the problem. She could have read a book by the available light. It's just that the man seemed transparent, and she could see the outline of the tree through him.

He was tall and muscular, with broad shoulders and long legs. He wore leather pants and a buckskin shirt, with leather fringes at the waist, the chest, and the shoulders. He wore a fur hat that looked like it was fashioned from a wolf hide. A leather shoulder strap held a satchel under his arm; a thick leather belt

20

around his waist supported a powder horn and a knife. His large-bore musket rested butt-first on the ground, the muzzle against his shoulder. He looked like someone from before the birth of the United States.

Madison was struck by his wooly dark beard and his piercing eyes, eyes that reflected deep emotions. He raised an eyebrow at Madison, and began talking in French.

She flicked her fingers at the apparition and commanded, "Speak the Common Tongue."

The man stepped back, almost bumping into the tree. "Oh ho! You are a witch, then?"

"No, I'm just Madison. I live here. Who are you?"

The man tapped his chest. "I am Étienne Carnot, the fur trader. Or at least, I was. It is an honor to meet you." He bowed his head.

She tried to figure out if she should curtsey, thought better of it, and settled for nodding back. It was unnerving, seeing the bark of the oak tree through him. It was as though he were a projection, yet in every other way he seemed quite real.

Is he an Escaped? But he spoke French, and none of the Escaped would speak an Earthly language.

He spoke again. "Sir...I mean, Madam!.....I am filled with embarrassment, I must apologize. You are dressed as a young man, but your face is as fair as a young lady. Please do not take offense!"

Madison realized the source of his confusion. "I am a girl, and I'm not a madam but a miss." She looked down at her long pants and t-shirt. "This is the current fashion."

I suppose I must look as odd to him as he does to me.

And he thought I was a boy. I could just die.

He wiped his brow of non-existent sweat. "Please forgive me. Miss Madison, you live here?" He looked beyond her at the tavern.

"Yes. This is my home."

21

"I had hoped for the gentleman of the house. I have a word I wish to share."

"Uncle Roddyn, the gentleman of the house, is busy right now." She usually didn't speak so formally, but she couldn't help copying his elegant speech.

"A pity. Well, then, have you a few minutes? I don't know how long I will be here." He turned, looking at the orchard and the stream. "Indeed, I am astonished to be here at all."

"Yes, I have time."

Nanny Bee stood motionless to one side, watching and listening.

He took a breath, and began his story.

"I sailed to the colonies from Le Havre in the Year of Our Lord 1609, and started a home in Quebec, just a small log house. Furs were my trade, and I came down with my buffalo musket looking for game. At a trading post I met a native named Watseka, a beautiful, fair-spoken woman. She said that she would introduce me to her brother who had 'big medicine' and could bring me many buffalo. I knew the native ways were fanciful, but she was a fine woman and I took her on as a guide.

"We followed a river south through low mountains, and then across country to here. I think she wanted to have her brother kill me and take my rifle, but as we traveled, our hearts began to speak to each other, and by the time we came to her brother's roundhouse, we were more than friends."

He cleared his throat and looked into Madison's eyes.

She nodded.

He pointed north to Mount Majestic. "That mountain, which she called O-da-lav, was covered with snow when we arrived. We approached from the east, and there was a native village here by this stream," he pointed towards the fishing stream behind the tavern, "but this was all woods except for the clearing where your home now sits and a huge circle of hides. Posts stood in the ground, and buffalo hides were stretched between them, sewn buffalo hides, so as to conceal what was in the circle.

22

"Watseka led me to her brother Nashashuk and introduced me as a fur trader. The French and the natives were on friendly terms; Nashashuk had a generous feast and a dance. We sat around the campfire and he told me stories about his fights with the Potawatomi and the Chippewa, and I told him bigger lies about my fights with the English. I didn't ask him what was inside the circle of buffalo hides, and he didn't tell me, but when night fell I could see a glow coming from it, as though a fire lay within, but it did not flicker like fire.

"That night I slept on my rifle. Watseka slept beside me, and I could tell from Nashashuk's eyes that he hated me for it."

Madison stared at the ghost of Étienne with fascination. He had lived here hundreds of years ago, and had had a love affair with a native woman. Early American history had just been books for Madison, pages without faces, but she could see by his worn rifle and his rugged countenance that he had lived that history.

"Morning came," he continued, "and I primed my musket just in case. I crawled out of the roundhouse to see that Nashashuk had put on ceremonial garments. He wore a set of plates on his chest that I swear were pure gold, and medicine bags on his arms, and paint on his face, not war paint, I know what that looks like, but this was colors on his forehead and under his eyes that showed that he was ready to commune with the Great Spirit.

"Watseka clutched my arm when she saw him dressed that way, and she whispered that I should leave her and go back to Quebec now, as fast as I could. Of course I did no such thing, and Nashashuk waved us forward to the buffalo hide circle.

"'Great hunter,' he said, 'I want to show you my big medicine.' He waved Watseka away, but she wouldn't go. She held on to my arm, and Nashashuk's eyes became like the ice on the mountain.

"The other natives gathered, and the women held their children close. Two men, also ceremonially dressed, stood beside the circle. Nashashuk pointed to them, and they pulled the hides aside, revealing the inside."

"*Mon Dieu!* I have never seen such a thing, and my blood froze. There in a pit was...was..." He waved his hands, trying to frame his words. "Imagine a ball made of snakes, each as thick as a man's waist, but not snakes – ropes, intertwined, each one glowing with points of light like the stars overhead, and slowly shifting. It was as big as that building behind you and I could not tell if I was gazing into heaven or hell, but it was all I could do to remain on my feet, and I am not a cowardly man.

"Nashashuk stepped up to the giant ball and turned towards us. He raised his hands, and lightning leaped into the cloudless sky, or from the sky into his hands, I could not tell which. I hefted my musket, as I could tell he meant me no good. No man with eyes burning with such hatred has ever done an act of kindness.

"He rubbed his hands together, gathering lightning, his teeth bared. Then he extended his arms and threw a bolt of lightning across the clearing at me and it would have been my death, but Watseka jumped in front of me and she took the brunt of it. She cried out and fell dead instantly.

"'No!' cried Nashashuk. For a moment I thought he would go to his dead sister and let me depart, but he raised his hands over his head and drew lightning again.

"I lifted my buffalo musket and fired. I had a reputation for my eye, and my shot was true. The ball hit him directly on one of the gold plates on his chest.

"He screamed and fell backwards, thrown by the impact. He landed on his back against one of the glowing ropes, and suddenly he seemed to slow down. I have never seen such a strange thing; he sank into the glowing rope like a ship sinking into a burning sea. The last I saw of Nashashuk was his hands.

"The strange ball shrank then, I don't know why. It settled down in the pit until it was a third of its original size. The natives drew back from it as though it frightened them.

"Watseka was dead. I could do nothing for her. I bowed my head to say a prayer for her heathen soul, but that was my

24

mistake. A young warrior had come up behind me, and he struck me on my head with his *tamahak,* killing me instantly.

"He scalped me, and the women buried my body where I lay. I know this because I chose to see it, because I chose to remain for a time." Étienne looked at Madison as though to see whether she disbelieved him. She nodded, and he continued. "The buffalo hide circle was closed, and the tribe gathered their belongings and moved on, except for a medicine woman that had built her little roundhouse next to the circle.

"A squirrel came and buried an acorn over my chest, and a hawk captured the squirrel in spring before it returned to claim it. The acorn sprouted, and this oak grew." Étienne looked up at the branches. "It has absorbed my heart, and sent its roots into my bones. I'm part of the tree now, at least my mortal remains are. This tree is not a normal tree."

He sighed, and looked at Madison as though he had set down a burden. "Now you know my story, Miss Madison. You should know two more things. First, I don't know why I was brought here now, at this time. I was....I was..." He stared into the distance. "I was learning how stars began their songs. Yes. That was it. But I got interrupted and found myself here. Something has changed. I don't know what, but something has changed." He lifted his rifle and let it rest on his shoulder. "I felt I needed to share my story. But this tree, Mademoiselle. That was the other thing. Do not trust this tree. It has my bones in it. Leave it be."

He exhaled. "I am done."

"Um...thank you?" Madison half-curtseyed.

His eyes moved beyond her. "I see the man of the house has arrived. You will have to tell him my story. My time is past." He squinted. "Are those Prussians beside him?"

Madison turned around. Uncle Roddyn had come out the back door, followed by the two bikers. They were staring at the ghost of Étienne. "I don't know."

He turned towards the orchard, and his voice softened. "Ah, and look yonder. Watseka calls to me."

Madison turned. In front of the rows of blossoming trees stood the outline of a woman in an ankle-length fringed leather dress, her hair in braids, one on either side of her head. The transparent woman lifted her hand silently, her face glowing from the radiance of her smile.

Étienne moved past Madison, not making a sound. He walked across the lawn, and not a blade of grass stirred. Watseka put out her hands, and Étienne dropped his rifle and grasped her hands with his. As they came together, they faded out of sight.

"What was that?" asked Roddyn as he walked up to Madison.

"The ghost of an old fur hunter that lived hundreds of years ago. He told me..." She wiped her eyes. "...He told me that before he died he saw a bright glowing ball, right there where the tavern sits, and he said that for some reason he was called back here to tell us about it, and to tell us his story. He was buried where this oak tree stands."

"He said this?"

"Yes. He was French. And that woman by the orchard was the Indian woman he loved."

The two bikers looked at each other, their eyes large. Nanny Bee pointed towards the orchard. "He left something lying on the ground."

They walked to where Nanny Bee had pointed, and there on the ground lay the pale transparent form of the buffalo musket. Nanny Bee picked it up and handed it to Roddyn.

Madison reached out her hand and stroked it. It was as though the rifle was made of down or thistle and she could see through it like glass, yet it did not bend. The bikers ran their fingers down the muzzle in wonder. "May I hold it?" Mitch asked.

Roddyn passed him the rifle, but even as he grasped it, it evaporated into mist and disappeared.

26

Chapter Four

Uncle Roddyn explained to Mitch and Penny as they went back inside the tavern that The Padded Cell had its ghosts just like many an old house and that they could travel to Baltimore or Gettysburg or Atlanta and get tours of other ghosted buildings.

"So you've seen things like that before?" Mitch asked, sitting at a booth and nursing another light beer. Penny stuck with ginger ale.

"Oh, once or twice, sure." Roddyn stroked his thick mustache. "This place goes way back. During the Civil War, troops from both sides came through here; I think this was used for a hospital once. If you believe in ghosts, some of the soldiers who died might still be hanging around."

"If I believe in ghosts?" Mitch snorted. "Madison has an afternoon chat with a dead fur trader and you say 'if?'"

"Well…"

"And the thing is, everything I've heard about ghosts, and I've never seen one before, is that you can't touch them. They're just spirit. But that gun of his, I could actually feel it, and then it just wasn't there, as though he'd taken it back or something. That really shook me up."

"Yes," said Roddyn, "I'd say he was more than an ordinary ghost."

"Last year when we tended bar, we didn't see anything unusual," said Penny, "or the year before that."

Mitch laughed. "Parties drive away spooks. Isn't that right, Madison?"

She shrugged.

A couple of patrons came in, and Roddyn went to take care of them. Mitch drained his bottle and shook his head. It had gotten dark out, and the hairy-armed cook was making the last of her burgers and fries. Pinhead had gone to his room upstairs to sleep, and Nanny Bee had retired to her closet. The bikers were seated next to Emtianal's booth – he was playing solitaire – and Madison was on a chair she had dragged up and turned backwards so that she was straddling it. She had trouble sitting like a lady.

Earlier, she had retold Étienne's story to Roddyn and the bikers. She shortened one part, though; she did not describe the glowing ball, the one with points of lights in it that moved like stars. She simply said that there was a "bright light" in the pit, and that Nashashuk had fallen into the pit when he had been shot. She looked at Uncle Roddyn when she mentioned the "bright light" and he nodded slightly at her. He understood. One never told everything that happened at The Padded Cell.

She was anxious for the tavern to empty so she could discuss with Uncle Roddyn what Étienne had told her. Unfortunately, she would have to wait until tomorrow. There would be customers from now until one a.m., and she was expected to go to her room by ten thirty.

Mitch finished his bottle, dropped a tip on the table and said goodnight to Madison. He and Penny went outside to start up their Electra Glides and head home. "I'll take care of it," said Madison to Roddyn. She rubbed her fingertips together under the table, and fired magic in their direction so that the bikes would start. Motors that close to the tavern wouldn't start without help.

She kept the magic flowing until the throaty sound of their bikes faded. Then she pushed her chair back to where it belonged, said goodnight to Emtianal, and waved to Uncle Roddyn. She went upstairs to her room to find out who had committed the murder on the Orient Express.

The ending surprised her.

It was Friday, the day of the Vernal Equinox celebration. Madison pulled on her work pants and a t-shirt that said, "I'm smiling. This should scare you." She rushed through her chores, showered, put on clean pants, stared at Emily Dickinson until she gave up, drew several sketches of Mount Majestic exploding into a volcano, and managed to lose herself in the process of making a pepper jack tomato soup. Pinhead, having put on an apron, grated the cheese and diced the tomatoes.

While the soup simmered, she stirred up a vanilla cake mix and put it into the oven to bake. She thought of last year's Equinox party when she had met a boy, Corey Mullins. He was sixteen, and he danced with her to some of the old songs played by the Jug and Fiddle band. She remembered his fun smile, his dark eyes, his spiky hair, and his necklace made of shells and silver skulls. He had come with his parents, and she had had a great time. He gave her a quick hug at the end of the last dance; she had trouble sleeping afterward.

Corey might come again. She had been reviewing some dance steps, but she regretted not having TV or the ability to visit local dances so she could see how people her age – well, Corey's age – really danced. The last thing she wanted was to look dorky. But the whole Equinox party had an old time flavor to it, like a historic recreation, so she wouldn't look silly when she danced the old dances.

She pulled her cake out of the oven and set it on a rack to cool, and then began filling orders for sandwiches. Pinhead dropped his apron in a hamper and changed to gardener's gloves and a sunhat. He headed out the front door to clear leaves from the beds where green rolls of hosta were just beginning to push their way above ground. Regulars waved at Pinhead, who always waved back, but a passerby looking for directions stopped and stared when he saw him. As Uncle Roddyn said, Pinhead was startling.

Madison finished at two o'clock and put away the mustard jar, mayonnaise, bread, and what was left of the sliced meats. As she was putting a layer of canned chocolate frosting on her birthday cake, she was surprised to find Pinhead at the back door, his gloved finger in his mouth. He still had on the sunhat, but he was swaying as he did when indecisive or upset.

"What's up?" she asked him as she dropped the spatula into the sink and removed her apron.

He pulled his finger from his mouth and said, "The tree is bad."

"What?"

What did he mean...oh! Étienne had said that the oak tree was not to be trusted, whatever that meant.

Pinhead repeated, "The tree is bad."

"The big oak tree out back?"

He nodded.

"Well, let's go see what's bad about it."

She was not concerned about any naughty tree. There was a sharp axe in the storage room, and Pinhead's woodsman hat. If necessary, the tree could be taken down, though it would take a day, maybe two, to get through the hardwood trunk with an axe.

She stepped out onto the porch – it was a cloudy day with the smell of rain in the air – and began walking towards the west corner of the tavern.

"Oh!" She stopped suddenly.

The oak tree had moved. It no longer stood a hundred yards to the west of the tavern, as it always had. It was closer by half.

Okay. That's bad.

She shivered. Étienne's ghost had warned her about the tree. Stay away from it, he had said. Do not trust it.

30

She walked to the tree and circled it, keeping her distance. Tolkien wrote about trees that would grasp and strangle. The oak, however, was quiet and motionless, at least for the moment, and hardly seemed likely to attack her.

And yet it had moved.

She walked to where it had stood for as long as she could remember, and there was a depression. Grass covered the area, but the ground was rough and uneven, and there was a trail of roughness that led to where the tree now stood. Sometime in the night, it had traveled towards the tavern.

"This tree is Escaped," said Pinhead, startling her.

"What?"

Pinhead held the sunhat on his head as he looked up into the branches. "The squirrel that carried its acorn was Escaped, too. This oak is a bad tree. It's wrong."

Madison stepped back a few more paces. So the tree was an Escaped? What if she flicked a Common Tongue spell at it? But it wasn't talking, and the Common Tongue spell wouldn't make a tree talk English if it wasn't talking already. Probably.

Nanny Bee walked up to them from the shed. "I see the tree decided to travel."

Madison chewed her lip as she looked at Nanny. Nanny Bee had her own perceptions. She looked so normal that most people never looked at her twice, but that was the odd thing about her. Her face was the average of all women, symmetrical and pretty in a plain sort of way.

"Decided?"

"It certainly moved by itself," said Nanny. "There are no tracks, no shovel marks, and its roots are deep in the earth right now. It moved last night and it isn't moving during the day, at least not now, not that I can tell."

"But why did you say it *decided* to move?"

Nanny Bee looked back to where the tree used to stand. "Because it has always stood in that place, and now it has moved. I don't know why it moved. But there must be a why."

31

"Étienne said he didn't know why *he* was drawn back here, but he said that something had changed. I think we need to call Uncle Roddyn. This is something the Caretaker needs to know about."

Nanny Bee nodded agreement, but her eyes looked at her with an enigmatic expression. Madison had the feeling that Nanny knew more than she was saying.

Madison called Uncle Roddyn, who was restocking the shelves under the bar and making sure that there was ice for the Equinox party. He came out the back door wiping his hands on his bartender's apron and muttering, "Trees don't just get up and walk, you know." But he stopped muttering when he saw the oak less than fifty yards from the corner of the tavern. "Well, I'll be." He circled the tree carefully, as Madison had done, and looked at the trail of rough sod behind it.

"What do you think?"

"It sure looks like an ordinary tree to me. I don't know, though." He tilted his head and studied the branches. "See any birds' nests up there?"

It was spring and birds were nesting in the orchard, nesting under the eaves, and nesting anywhere else there seemed to be a decent spot. Try as she might, though, she didn't see any nests in the oak. "No, but nests aren't always easy to see."

"What do you think, Pinhead?"

Pinhead stood further away from the tree than Madison and Roddyn. "The tree is Escaped, and it's a bad tree. It's not a pure tree. I would be afraid to cut it down." He put his finger in his mouth. "I don't know what to do."

Roddyn rubbed his jaw. "I think that this calls for some action. Pinhead, everybody, come with me."

"What?" asked Madison. "What are you going to do?"

"You'll see. Come inside by the cellar door." He went into the storage room, and came back out carrying a cardboard box labeled Monastery's Finest Vin Rosé. He opened it, pulled out a worn white lab coat, and shook it. "Pinhead, take off your hat and gloves and put this on."

"Okay." As Pinhead slipped on the lab coat, Roddyn pulled out a pair of thick black plastic eyeglasses and a wig.

"You're kidding," said Madison.

"Not at all. We need Pinhead's insight." He helped Pinhead slip on the eyeglasses – they only had plastic for the lenses – and adjusted the wig of wild gray hair on his narrow head.

"One more touch." Roddyn reached into the box and pulled out a couple of old pens. He tucked them into the pocket of the lab coat, and handed Pinhead an empty clipboard. "There."

"Uh-oh," said Pinhead. He stopped swaying, straightened up and took a deep breath. His eyes brightened and he spoke with clarity. "Ah, yes. Yes, indeed. Étienne's ghost was right. Things have changed."

"Tell us what's happening," said Uncle Roddyn.

Pinhead tucked the clipboard under his arm and put his hand on his forehead. "This is very painful. It makes my head hurt. But if you want to understand what is happening, I need to start from the beginning. I need to tell you where the pocket universe came from that lies in the cellar beneath this tavern."

Chapter Five

Standing between the bar and the cellar door, Pinhead put one arm behind his back and spoke in a professorial voice. "The pocket universe began as all other universes have begun – with a blossoming into existence. It expanded, spreading out its energy, lowering the temperature of the proto-elements until they separated from the plasma and become the lightest gases. Unevenness developed in the primal matter, clouds of density paving the way for the coalescence of material to form stars and planets."

I wish I understood what he was saying.

He raised a finger. "There was only one problem. Our universe was here first." He rubbed his round chin. "There was no room for the new universe to expand. Its cosmic constant shifted, its physics became modified. Whereas this universe we live in is still expanding, the pocket universe turned inward."

His small eyes blinked behind the plastic lenses. "Worlds formed, worlds with dense minerals like ours, worlds shaped and molded by the life that came forth. Time passes more rapidly on its worlds, and intelligence there can shape forces in what we call *magic*, pulling actuality from a thousand possibilities."

He rubbed the side of his head and winced. "There is an intelligence in each universe beyond our comprehension, an intelligence made up of all living things on all worlds. They evolved a truce, the two universes did, they settled on a balance, but then that balance was endangered when this planet Earth came swinging through the cosmos and captured the little universe. The boundaries became weaker, less clear.

"Nashashuk was not the first to discover it. There are many stories..." He stopped and wiped sweat from his face.

He won't be able to keep this up much longer. I hope he gets to the heart of it before he collapses.

"When Nashashuk fell into the pocket universe, it restored the balance somewhat. It shrank. But the worlds in that universe often come into contact with the brane boundary..."

"Brain?" asked Madison, and then immediately regretted it. She didn't want to prolong his pain.

"Brane. B. R. A. N. E." He looked at her like she was a dunce. "It is how the Escaped move into our universe, and it is how Nashashuk was taken in. But recently the balance has slipped again. Something has shifted. The pocket universe is expanding.

"In their worlds, the sky is different because the worlds are too close to each other. Sometimes an adventuresome being will climb to the highest mountain, and touch the sky, and find themselves in our world...." He put his hand on the edge of the bar and shuddered. "Like me."

"He needs to take off the costume," said Madison, but Roddyn raised his hand to silence her.

Pinhead looked at her in anguish, a drop of sweat rolling down his face. "The influence of the pocket universe is expanding because too many have Escaped into our world. That is why the tree woke up." His voice got louder. "The balance has tipped and needs to be restored or this world will be destroyed!" He dropped the clipboard and ripped off the wig. "No more!" he cried. "No more!" He tore the glasses from his face and staggered out the back door, flinging the lab coat aside.

"Well," said Roddyn, "that worked better than I had hoped."

"Worked?" Madison looked at him incredulously. "He looked like he was about to die!"

"Die? Faint, perhaps, but he was nowhere near death. It's an odd magic he has, but useful." He picked up the lab coat and retrieved the glasses. "We knew most of that, of course, but we need to be more diligent. That wandering tree out back is an Escaped, as is Pinhead."

"We're not going to send Pinhead back," said Madison firmly.

"No, no, I have no intention of sending Pinhead back, or Emtianal. The tree is a different matter, but I haven't any idea how to get the tree to contact a brane so it would return. It would certainly help matters if we could."

"Would the tree going back be enough to restore the balance?"

"I don't know." He sat down on a bar stool and stroked his mustache. "We can't just cut the tree into pieces and toss it in; I think it needs to be intact, alive. If it was just substance, if all we needed to do was to transfer matter, we could shovel in some rocks and be done with it."

She stared at the ornate mirror behind the bar and pondered. Certainly, letting any more Escaped wander loose would make things worse. But it might be cruel to push a creature through a brane into a world that was not their own. "What kind of place did Nashashuk wind up in, I wonder?"

"He might have wound up as a slave or as a god. More likely he wound up eating ferns and dodging bizarre creatures until he passed away, unless the world he entered had no atmosphere at all and he perished instantly."

She shivered.

"Now if you'll excuse me," said Roddyn, "I need to get ready for the Equinox party tonight. I'll think more on this later."

"Do you think that any bizarre creatures from the pocket universe ever wandered into our world? I mean, more bizarre than usual, more bizarre than the Rat Witch?"

"You mean like vampires, the Sasquatch, leprechauns, unicorns....?" He shrugged. "Who knows?"

"But they wouldn't have their magic if they moved away from here."

"That's right; the magic from the pocket universe doesn't extend very far. But some creatures might survive without magic just by their nature. I don't know, and I don't have time to think about it."

"I'll let you go get ready. Thank you for looking at the tree."

"Keep an eye on it, Maddy, but from a distance. We didn't learn much about it from Pinhead. I have no idea what it might do, but we've got to carry on like there's nothing unusual. Tomorrow, we'll deal with it. Just don't go out back after dark tonight. Stay inside."

Madison picked up the wig and clipboard and put them in the costume box. She put the box in the storeroom and went outside with Nanny Bee. Pinhead was lying face down in the grass, his arms covering his head. She patted him and told him that he was a good Pinhead, that everybody was happy with him, and that he should rest. He nodded and sniffed.

She smelled burgers and fries. The hairy-armed cook was making dinner. "I'm going to eat early, Nanny, and get ready for the party tonight."

"Okay, dear," Nanny Bee said, and headed towards the shed to fold laundry. Nanny said nothing about the oak tree; Nanny was not a worrier.

Madison had a light dinner – she was too anxious to eat more than one thin slice of her birthday cake – and then she ran upstairs and showered. In a little while she would have a chance to dance with Corey Mullins again! She shivered with excitement as she put on more crème rinse. And if she was lucky, he would hug her again. It didn't quite come up to the great romance stories, but for her it would be something exciting.

She tried to start a new novel, the first book of the *No. 1 Lady's Detective Agency*, but after the first chapter she set it aside and watched the sun set. The Equinox party wouldn't start until after dark, although people were starting to filter in. She sat at her vanity and looked at herself in the mirror. Her hair was almost dry, and she brushed it aggressively, willing it to be beautiful, soft and silky, not the rebellious brown tangle it usually was.

She heaved a huge sigh, and looked at her face morosely. Not enough cheekbones, as usual. Nose not perky enough. As usual. Eyes too, too....she leaned closer...too green tonight. Well, green was okay. Better than gray, like they were yesterday.

She pulled out a drawer and took out some makeup. Mrs. Regan had snuck it past Uncle Roddyn. "I thought you might enjoy these things, dear," she said. "It won't be long now until you'll be a young woman."

Only like, forever.

She looked at the lipstick. It was bright red.

There are lots of different shades. How do I know if this is right for me?

She shrugged, and colored her mouth. Then she rubbed it off vigorously, and tried again, keeping more carefully within the boundaries of her lips. This time they didn't look so Barnum and Bailey, just....red.

She put powder all over her face – it seemed a bit pale – and then rouged her cheeks.

Should I pluck my eyebrows? And if so...how much? And what shape?

She yanked out one hair and it hurt, so she decided that her eyebrows were just fine the way they were. She found a thick pencil labeled "eyebrow pencil" and she darkened her eyebrows. Circus music began playing in her head again and she wiped off some of the color with a tissue.

Eyeliner next.

Then some eye shadow.

Egyptian. Now she looked Egyptian. She used more tissue and tried again.

She turned off the overhead light and turned on her nightstand light.

38

That looks better. It won't be bright down there anyway.

She put on her blue party dress, which had sleeves and reached to her knees – Uncle Roddyn wouldn't let her have anything short, and Mrs. Regan never brought anything daring – and she looked at herself in the mirror.

She was still a skinny fourteen, in spite of her stupid birthday cake. Corey would be a year older, but she wouldn't be.

She growled in exasperation and yanked several tissues from the box and stuffed them down her front. She grabbed another handful and stuffed them down the other side, and tried to make them look symmetrical. After a bit of tucking, she looked like she actually had a shape. Sort of.

There. Now I won't look like so much like a little girl.

She looked at herself in the mirror, and spun around, excited.

Nanny Bee and Sheryl stood in the doorway, their arms folded.

"Ack!" Madison sat down on her bed.

Nanny shook her head. "Take them out."

"What?" Madison lifted her chin defiantly. "I'm ready to go to the party."

Sheryl smiled. "Nanny Bee's right, Madison. Good try, but that's not the effect you want."

"But…"

"Trust me, girl." She motioned for Madison to sit down at her vanity again. "We can do better than that."

Reluctantly Madison pulled out the hidden tissues, and wiped her face clean. Nanny Bee went downstairs to get another box of tissues from the storage room.

"Now look here," said Sheryl, leaning over her, "you've got a very pretty face, and all you need to do is highlight it a little." She yanked a fresh tissue from the new box Nanny brought up and handed it to Madison. "Clean your eyes better. Use some cold cream; you look gothic."

"Maybe I *want* to look gothic."

"No, you don't. If you're trying to look nice for some young man at the party tonight, you don't want to look like the living dead."

Madison grumbled and removed the last of the makeup, irritating her eyes, and then tried to hold still as Sheryl fussed over her. Sheryl brushed Madison's hair in a different direction, reducing the wildness of it, and then put the lightest bit of rouge on her cheeks and smoothed it out. "Nothing on your lips, certainly not that horrid color. You've got healthy lips."

I don't want "healthy" lips, I want lips that drive men mad and make them swoon at my feet. Or at least that make them want to look at me a second time.

Sheryl leaned back and nodded at Madison in the mirror's reflection. "There."

"There? But I don't even look like I have makeup on!"

"That's when you know you've done it right. Trust me."

Madison bit her tongue and didn't point out that Sheryl was single. She sighed. She was being ganged up on, and there was nothing she could....

The window shattered, the curtain tore, and a branch pushed into the room.

Sheryl screamed.

Madison jumped away from the vanity and pressed her back against the wall, as far away from the moving branch as possible. The leafy branch opened and closed like a human hand, and she pictured herself being grasped and crushed by it. Certainly anything that could smash through double-pane glass like it was paper would have strength behind it.

"Speak the common tongue," she said in a quaver, and flicked her fingers at it.

The branch slammed down onto her bed, breaking one of the bed legs, and a reedy voice came scratching into her brain.

Noooo speeeaaaaakkkk. Nooooo tonnnnnggggggue.

40

"What is that thing?" gibbered Sheryl as she clung to Nanny Bee, who was blocking the door and keeping Sheryl from running out in hysterics.

"You're safe," said Nanny Bee calmly. "It's just a branch."

"Why are you moving?" Madison asked the tree out loud. She didn't know if the tree could read her thoughts or not.

Caaaannnn nnnooottt slleeeeeeeeeeppp.

"Well, I can't sleep either. What do you want?"

Doooo noooooottt wwaaannnnnttt. Toooo muuuuccchh nnnnnnnnnoooissssssssse.

Sheryl whimpered.

Can Sheryl hear the tree? Probably not.

Madison pointed her fingers towards the tree and threw magic at it. "Move away from the house and go to sleep!" She used both hands. "Sleep!"

Haaaate nnnnnoooisssse. Haaaaate liiiiivviinnnngg thiiiiiinnnnggsssss.

The branch pulled back out the window, dragging more glass with it. From downstairs she could hear the drum set of the Jug and Fiddle band pounding away, and the chatter of voices. If anyone had heard Sheryl scream, they weren't investigating.

"What was that? What just happened?" cried Sheryl, pulling away from Nanny Bee.

Madison looked out the window, and could see the oak tree inching away into the darkness. "There's a rotten tree outside and the wind blew a branch into the window."

"I didn't hear any wind," said Sheryl, her eyes white. "You were waving your hands at it and talking to it! What were you doing?"

"It only took a gust to break that branch. I knew it was rotten and we should have cut it down sooner. You could see how it was rolling around before it fell back out." She cleared her throat. "I said a good luck charm that an old lady taught me. I know it was silly of me but I guess it worked."

41

"I'll cover the broken window with plastic and we can fix it in the morning," said Nanny Bee. "It sounds like the party has started."

"Well, that near scared me to death." Sheryl looked warily at the window. "It broke your bed. Where will you sleep?"

"I can pull the mattress onto the floor." She shrugged. "Really, the only problem is that poor Uncle Roddyn has to repair the window. I told him he should have cut that branch."

Sheryl shivered. "I need a stiff drink." She edged out the door.

"You handled that well," said Nanny quietly, so that only Madison could hear.

"Thanks. I don't know if Sheryl bought my explanation." She wrinkled her face in thought. "It's angry, that tree. No wonder Pinhead said it was bad."

"Are you up to joining the party? Your heart is still pounding."

"I'll settle down. I think I'd feel safer down there than up here."

"I'll stay up tonight and keep watch."

"Thank you. It'll help knowing you're around."

She brushed her party dress smooth and exhaled, forcing herself to relax. It was time to make an entrance, a quiet entrance, and hope that Corey Mullins was there and that he would dance with her and that she could forget about walking trees that hated the living.

Chapter Six

Madison started down the stairs, savoring the party atmosphere. The Jug and Fiddle band was in the alcove that doubled as a stage, though the five man band just barely fit. They used the tavern's old upright piano, and brought their own drum set and other instruments. The old musicians were versatile enough to play rock, jazz, swing, klezmer, square dance, or polka. They even played the traditional Bunny Hop, which some people had to drag their partners into joining.

A blonde singer usually started the evening with some rock tunes, but as the crowd got happier, more singers would join in. By 1 a.m. the band was at its loudest and mostly out of tune, but no one cared.

The Vernal Equinox celebration at the Padded Cell was one of those peculiar holidays that develops spontaneously. The Equinox party had no competition and the group of regulars was still small enough that they fit into the tavern, as long as some were content to be in the far booths by the kitchen. At six o'clock the cook shut down the kitchen so the dining booths could hold more people.

Uncle Roddyn had Pinhead haul in extra ice, and for the evening, the Wine Cellar was actually a wine cellar. People ordered expensive drinks and Roddyn juggled glasses and bottles like he had four arms.

Madison stopped halfway down the stairs and looked over the room. Mitch and Penny were there, and Sheryl with a drink in her hand and a too-wide smile on her face. In his booth, Emtianal was sipping an ice-filled lemonade through a straw and socializing.

The band finished playing *Stand By Your Man* and everyone applauded the singer. She sat down on a bar stool while the band launched into Jimmy Dorsey's *Clarinet Polka*.

The dance floor thinned out; not many people knew how to polka, but some went ahead and danced anyway. Madison walked carefully around the edge of the crowd; some weren't dancing all that steady.

She spied Corey Mullins in a booth near the kitchen where most of the kids sat and her heart began racing again. She recognized his light brown spiky hair and his dark eyes; he had on a black turtleneck under a sport coat, and around his neck stretched a necklace of shark's teeth. He looked a little taller and a little more muscular than last year. She pictured getting a hug from him and swallowed.

Courage, Madison.

She walked up to his booth with a smile and said, "Hi, Corey!"

Then she noticed the girl sitting with him.

The girl had short blonde hair and creamy white skin, and the spaghetti straps of her dark red dress emphasized her flawless shoulders. She had quite clearly not needed to resort to stuffing Kleenex down her front. She looked up at Madison, her sculpted eyebrows raised.

Madison froze.

Corey smiled and stood up, hampered by the booth's table. "Hey! It's, uh, the bartender's daughter. Right? What was your name again?" He thrust out his hand, and she managed to put her hand into his. He shook it and let go.

That girl he's with, that woman, is gorgeous, and my hand was limp as spaghetti when he shook it, and she's got a figure and I don't and and he didn't remember me and he's seventeen now and I'm still fourteen...

44

"I'm Maddy. Hi." Then she remembered that she had already said hi. But that was just to Corey.

Corey waved his hand towards the blonde. "This is my friend, Jennifer. Jennifer, this is Maddy, she's the bartender's daughter."

"Niece," said Madison, extending her hand towards the woman. "He's my uncle."

"Hiya," Jennifer said with a half-smile. She glanced towards Corey as though wondering why she was meeting this little girl.

"We danced last year," said Madison. "Corey and me." She cleared her throat. "Corey and I."

Jennifer nodded, her smile unchanged.

"Yeah, I remember that," said Corey, sitting back down again. "Hey, if I get a chance, I'll dance another one with you. You know, you haven't changed a bit." He smiled as though it was a compliment. Jennifer leaned a little closer to him.

"Thanks," said Madison. "It's, like, my birthday today and I'm, um, fifteen. I'll be around." Madison glanced about as though looking for other friends, trying to ignore Jennifer's assessing gaze. "Nice to meet you. I gotta run."

She smiled and backed up, trying to remember how people separated from each other at parties, and then turned and walked away, her face reddening. She heard Jennifer laugh.

There was room beside Emtianal, and she sat down, her eyes threatening to betray her with tears.

Emtianal leaned towards her. "I see that the young man you danced with last year has a girl."

"Yes." She stared at the tabletop and folded her hands in her lap. The band started playing *The Tennessee Waltz*.

Emtianal whispered so only she could hear. "They move on, the people from outside." He tapped his fingers on the table. "Do you know the words to this song?"

She shook her head.

Emtianal sang in a hoarse whisper, "I remember the night and the Tennessee Waltz, now I know just how much I have lost. Yes, I lost my little darlin', the night they were playing, the beautiful Tennessee Waltz."

She leaned against his shoulder. "I didn't lose anything, Emtianal. I just wanted to dance with him." She heaved a deep sigh. "Why did that stupid girl have to be sitting with him?"

"Because he brought her. They make a fine couple. See them dancing?"

She looked where Emtianal pointed, and saw them doing the waltz. The woman – the high school girl – was graceful. Maybe more slinky than graceful.

Her eyes wandered off of them, and she looked at the other couples. Some were just friends, some much more than friends, some had years of marriage behind them.

She didn't need a boyfriend. But it would have been nice to dance.

Blinking back tears, Maddy noticed that someone else was sitting alone in a corner near the back door, in the shadows. He caught Madison's attention by the way he was sitting; stiff, his hands on his knees, his back against the wall. He looked like someone on the edge of the party who was afraid to join in.

Should I go over and say hello to him? Maybe he would like someone to talk to? But what if he told me to go away and leave him alone?

Do I really want to get rejected again tonight? I'll just stay here. It's safer.

The man leaned forward and looked towards the bar.

The man was Corey.

But it couldn't be! Corey was dancing with that Jennifer girl!

She scanned the couples until she found Corey and Jennifer, and then looked back at the man in the corner. He had the same light brown spiked hair, the same black turtleneck and jacket, and the same necklace of shark's teeth.

46

Okay. I'm guessing this is another pocket universe thing, and Uncle Roddyn is as busy as can be so it's going to be up to me. Pinhead was right. Things are getting out of hand.

For some reason, she seemed much more comfortable confronting someone from another world than a boy and his girlfriend from her own. She stood up.

"Careful, Madison," whispered Emtianal. "I see what you see, and it might not be safe."

She rubbed her hands together and felt the magic. "I know, I know. He's probably an Escaped. But Uncle Roddyn can't deal with him right now. I'll be careful." She walked around the edge of the room to where the copy of Corey was sitting, and said, "Hello."

He stiffened and stared at her, saying nothing.

"Hello. My name's Madison." She smiled, trying to reassure him.

"Hello," he said.

"How are you enjoying the party?"

"Hello?" He looked at her without comprehension. His eyes were dark, like Corey's, but the edges were more crinkled, like an older man inhabited them. He slid forward on his chair, putting some of his weight on his feet.

She was afraid that he would bolt out the back door, so she flicked her fingers at him and whispered, "Speak the Common Tongue."

He remained silent, but his eyes began flickering around the room. Many people were talking over the loudness of the band, and she guessed that now he could understand them.

"My name's Madison," she said again.

"I am sorry," he said. "I did not hear you. I greet you."

She nodded, and looked back to see what Corey and his date were doing. They were dancing dangerously near herself and the stranger.

"Can you change this to white?" she asked, poking his turtleneck where it stretched across his chest.

47

He jerked back, startled, and then eased forward again. The turtleneck faded to white.

"Good. I thought you could. Otherwise you wouldn't have been able to copy Corey. Now your hair. Make it dark brown, and make it a little longer and smoother. No spikes."

He looked up at her as his hair changed, and a half-smile crept onto his lips. "You are not surprised that I can do this?"

"I'm not surprised at much of anything. Now the necklace. Make it, like, a gold chain...no, not so thick...listen, can you just make it disappear?" The necklace vanished.

His face changed also; the nose increased in size, the planes of this cheeks strengthened, and his skin became darker and smoother. "You want me not to look like that boy. I understand."

If I had his ability to change myself, I wouldn't have needed those tissues and Jennifer would have had some competition.

She grabbed a momentarily empty chair from a table. She almost sat backwards in it before she realized that she was in a dress, so she turned it around and sat like a lady. "You came here from a different place, I think. I'm going to guess that you found yourself in this crowd of people, and wanted to fit in. Am I right?"

He nodded, looking around. "Am I in danger here?"

"Oh, heavens, no, this is just a party. But if someone saw you looking exactly like someone else here, you would have everyone looking at you and asking a lot of questions."

"What do you want from me?"

"Nothing. For now, just try to fit in. Later, I'll show you how to get back to your world."

His eyes narrowed. "Later."

"That's right. Later."

Until the party's over, I can't guide him back to the pocket universe, and it's obvious he came from there. Uncle Roddyn's using the wine cellar and can't shift it. And this person didn't look too anxious about returning to his home world. I might need Uncle Roddyn's help.

The stranger shifted in his seat.

48

"Are you thirsty or hungry?" Madison asked. "Are you okay?"

He lifted his chin. "I have no needs. Why are they doing that dance? What do they hope to gain?"

"Gain?"

"Do they dance for harvest, or for protection? Are they going to war?"

The waltz finished, and the band took a moment's intermission to sip their drinks. Uncle Roddyn and Mitch redoubled their efforts at serving the crowd that moved to the bar, and Penny circulated, clearing tables. "No, they are dancing just for fun. They are not trying to cause anything."

"The men dance with the women. Perhaps it is for fertility."

"No, they're not dancing for fertility." She felt her face get warm. "It's the Vernal Equinox party, you know, in spring when the days are as long as the nights. They are all, like, getting to know each other. They're socializing."

He nodded. "Fertility."

I don't think I like him, whatever he is. He didn't believe what I said. Maybe it's because I'm a girl; some guys are like that.

The band started up the Isley Brothers' version of *Twist and Shout*. A few brave couples, including Corey and his date, joined the older patrons in the knee-twisting dance. Corey had probably forgotten her already, and she was going to be a wallflower for the rest of the evening, watching over the Escaped. There were no other single teenage boys in the crowd, and she wasn't about to dance with any of the half-drunk older men.

"That is loud music," said the stranger, leaning towards her so that he could be heard.

"Yes, it is. What's your name?"

"My name." He looked at the floor. "Call me Odalav."

Why does that sound familiar?

"Odalav. Yes, it's a dance called the Twist. It's simple. There's nothing to it."

He nodded. "I can see that. The drums are good, but those other things…"

She tried to picture how the band must sound to someone who had never heard such instruments, but couldn't. Odalav seemed harmless. He hadn't attacked anyone, or bolted in fear out the back door. If she could keep him occupied until the evening was over, perhaps she could guide him back to the brane of his own world without fuss.

"Do you think you could do that?" she asked, looking out at the dance floor.

"Play the drums?"

"No. Do that dance. It's called the Twist."

"Is it required?"

I don't want to go through my birthday – what there is of it – without a dance, even if it is with a strange being from another world.

And it would keep him occupied.

"No, it's not required, but if you just stand there and do that," she pointed to a young couple twisting away energetically, "no one will look at you."

"Why would I do that?"

"Please? I helped you avoid attention. It would be a favor for me."

He looked around the room. "There are many sitting down."

"We can dance right here near the bar where it's dark." She ventured another half-truth. "If you dance, you'll fit in better."

He stood up, looking at his outfit and shaking his arms. "If I must dance your Twist, I must. But I do not understand why you would choose to dance in this clothing. It just gets in the way."

She moved so that her back was to the bar; she wanted to see what the other dancers were doing. "Just move like I do. Watch me."

After a few false starts she got into it, moving her hips and legs just like Corey and Jennifer. Odalav waved his arms

50

awkwardly and turned side to side until she coached him how to swing his knees in a proper twist.

He kept his expression wary, but his movements settled down to something resembling a version of the '60's dance. Madison let herself get into it, enjoying the music and the fun of dancing with a group of people. She could almost pretend that she was at a dance with a date, a handsome young man from another universe.

Deep down inside, though, she didn't trust him. He wasn't as lost as he ought to be for someone who just left his universe behind.

The number ended all too soon, and when the band moved on to the *Electric Slide*, Odalav balked. He said it was too complicated and too silly. They sat down, and Madison got a couple of glasses of ice water from behind the bar.

Odalav took his glass without any thanks, and looked at it closely. He sipped the water, glared at the lemon perched on the edge, and then drained the glass. Madison was about to offer a refill when she realized that the room had grown suddenly quiet.

She looked over at the main door, and there stood a police officer in a pressed tan uniform, a pistol on his hip as well as a Taser, hand cuffs, pepper spray, and a couple of cell phones, all in black leather cases.

It was not Sheriff Carson.

He pulled off his sunglasses – Madison thought it odd that he would wear sunglasses at night, but she figured it was part of his style – and he looked at the band. "Don't stop," he said in a casual voice as he tucked the glasses precisely into his shirt pocket. "Sheriff Carson's on vacation for a week. I'm just doing his rounds."

The leader of the Jug and Fiddle band, an old round man with wispy gray hair, nodded politely at the officer and started the band back up, playing *The Devil Went Down to Georgia*. Madison grabbed Odalav's hand. "Come with me quick," she whispered, and led him down the side of the room to the dining area. They sat down at an empty booth.

The officer got a glass of Coke from Roddyn and sat at the bar for a minute, talking to him and glancing at the crowd. A few brave souls got up to dance, ignoring the Law in their midst.

Madison turned to Odalav, and he had on black sunglasses. "No!" she snapped. They vanished.

"He is a ruler," said Odalav. "He has power."

"He's a sheriff. They do law enforcement. He enforces the laws."

"Everyone is afraid of him."

She leaned towards Odalav, trying to speak quietly over the music. "They aren't afraid of him. Well, sort of. He can put someone in jail if they break the law."

"That is power."

"It's power in a good way. People trust the sheriffs."

"But they got quiet. They looked afraid."

She shook her head and took a sip of water. "They thought it might have been an emergency. We haven't seen this sheriff before. Usually it's Sheriff Carson that..." She paused. Someone was standing beside her table.

She looked up to see the new sheriff looking down at her, frowning. His nameplate said GAZZIO and his shoulder patch said SHARONVILLE POLICE. "May I see your drink, Miss?" he asked.

She hesitantly held up her glass, and he took it and sniffed. He set it back down and looked at Odalav. "And yours, sir?"

Madison lifted Odalav's empty glass, and the sheriff sniffed it also. "We're not drinking, officer," she said. "It's just water."

"You were behind the bar, Miss. The owner can lose his liquor license if he permits minors at the bar, whether they're drinking or not."

"I live here, officer. This is my home. I was just getting us some water because Uncle Roddyn's so busy."

Sheriff Gazzio scanned the room as he spoke. "That doesn't matter, Miss. If anyone underage goes from this dining area to the bar while it's open, they're breaking state law." He focused on her face again. "The bartender said that you're his niece, and that your name is Madison?"

"That's right." Out of the corner of her eye, she saw Odalav sitting motionless. She hoped that he wouldn't do something crazy like pulling a sword out of thin air and attacking the sheriff.

"I have a daughter that goes to Sharonville High. I've been to lots of assemblies and basketball games, and I don't remember seeing you."

"I'm being homeschooled."

"That would explain it." He scanned the dance floor again as he spoke. "Who is homeschooling you?"

"Uncle Roddyn."

"I see. How's that going?"

Madison felt herself getting upset. Sheriff Gazzio was getting too personal, and it was none of his business. "It's going great. I can name every president and vice president since 1776 and every state capitol and what each state is famous for...." She stopped and bit her tongue before she could add, *Can you?*

"No need to get defensive, Miss." Gazzio's smile was thin. "It's all part of my job. You and your friend have a good time. Just stay away from the bar, okay?"

"Yes, sir." She nodded, trying to control her attitude.

The sheriff circled around, nodded to the other couples, including Corey and Jennifer, and then he left the tavern.

The band played a little louder, and more people returned to the dance floor.

"He did not have a weapon," said Odalav.

"Oh, yes, he did. He had a gun on his hip." She wiped her brow. She hadn't realized how tense she was.

"It was small."

"It could kill you easily enough."

"I mustn't look like him?"

53

She spoke forcefully. "You must stay the way you are now, and you need to stay put. I'll bring you a snack from the kitchen and you can sit here until the party's over. Which won't be long now."

His eyes smoldered. He wasn't used to being spoken to in that manner, apparently.

Is it because I'm a girl? Or maybe because I don't have mandibles or fangs like his people might in their true form?

She turned on the light in the kitchen and threw a sandwich together, glancing at Odalav to make sure he didn't wander off. When she returned to the table, he inspected the sandwich with distaste, tore it apart, and ate the meat. She handed him some napkins for his hands and cleared the table.

The crowd thinned out, the band packed up their instruments, Mitch and Penny settled up and left, and soon Uncle Roddyn was locking the front door.

Odalav stood as Roddyn walked over to them. "What did the sheriff want?" Roddyn asked.

"Nothing." Madison got to her feet also. "He thought we might have been drinking. He sniffed our drinks."

"You need to be careful." He looked at Odalav appraisingly. "So, who is this gentleman?"

"This is Odalav, and he wandered into our world, it seems."

"Odalav." He nodded at the Escaped. "You can understand us, I take it?"

"This child has made it so. But I find your ways are different than my ways."

"Yes, I suppose you would."

Madison put her hand on Roddyn's arm. "Would you shift the cellar so it shows the way back?"

"Yes." He looked at Odalav and tilted his head. "Come with me."

Odalav hesitated, looking from Roddyn to Madison and back again. Then he nodded without speaking, and walked with them to the cellar entrance.

Roddyn pushed the cellar door closed, grasped the carved letters that said WINE CELLAR and slid them to one side. The basement rumbled, and when he opened the door again, a bright golden glow came from the bottom of the stairs.

"No!" said Odalav sharply. "I will not return there!" He stepped back and glared at them.

"But this is your world," said Roddyn, pointing to the golden surface at the bottom of the stairs. "It is where you belong. You will better off there."

Odalav raised both arms over his head, and shook his hands. A ripple passed down his body, and his clothes changed. His hair was now shoulder length and black, his chest was bare except for a breastplate made of squares of beaten gold, and he wore a breechclout and leather leggings. A tomahawk was stuck into his beaded belt, and his face was painted.

Madison suddenly made the connection, and she gasped.

"My name is Nashashuk!" the native cried. He stabbed his finger downwards and electricity sparked from his fingertip. "And THIS is my world!"

Chapter Seven

Nashashuk!

Madison stepped back, her fingers gathering magic. She remembered Étienne's story about Nashashuk, how the native had cast lightning from his hands, and how the ball from Étienne's musket against Nashashuk's breastplate had knocked him back into the pocket universe.

"It's you!" she said. "Watseka was your sister!"

"Yes! How have you heard of me?"

From the corner of her eye, she could see Uncle Roddyn sliding cautiously towards the bar. "I heard about you from the man she loved, and I know that you killed Watseka!"

He grimaced. "An accident! That demon, that Frenchman, bewitched her. He was not of our tribe! He should have been the one to die!" Nashashuk glanced at Roddyn, and back to her. "I fell into another world when he shot me, a harsh world, a cruel world, where the spirits were unknown to me, the plants, the creatures, all wrong. A lesser man would not have survived." He crossed his arms over his chest, lifting his chin proudly. "I, Nashashuk, survived. For a thousand years I have lived in that world, alone."

Time moves faster in those worlds, Pinhead said.

"Then I saw the sky change," he continued. "It lowered until it touched a distant mountain, and I ran for a day and a night until I could climb and touch the sky. And now I am here, and I will not go back. This is my home, and now I will live the life that was robbed from me."

56

She looked into the cellar at the brane, the boundary to the other universe. It bulged halfway up the steps. It was growing. The balance between universes was severely off.

He must go back. Yes, this was his world once, but he is throwing off the balance and he killed his own sister when he tried to kill an innocent man. I have no sympathy for him.

Uncle Roddyn, frowning under his thick mustache, swung a double-barreled shotgun over the bar and aimed it at Nashashuk. "Your story touches me deeply, but I'm afraid you have no choice. You must return."

Without warning, Nashashuk turned and thrust his hands at Roddyn. "Never!" Lightning crackled from his hands. Roddyn put up a hand defensively, but the flash of electricity knocked him back against the shelf in front of the ornate mirror, and he and the bottles on the glass shelf crashed to the ground.

"No!" cried Madison.

Nashashuk turned back towards her and hurled more lightning. Madison put up her hands, palms first. A screen of magic appeared in front of her that divided the lightning and made it pass harmlessly on either side.

I didn't know I could do that...is Uncle Roddyn dead!?

She tried desperately to keep her mind clear as she stumbled backwards towards the rear door. Nashashuk was murderous. He had killed his own sister; he had tried to kill Étienne. He would kill again, just to stay in this world.

Once more Nashashuk struck, and again her magic shielded her. She shoved the back door open with her hand and ran into the darkness, hoping to escape, but she only got a few steps before she heard Nashashuk coming out the door after her.

I must not have my back to him. I'll be defenseless.

She turned just in time to fend off another lightning bolt. She took a deep breath, marshaled her magic, and thrust her hands at him. "Sleep!" she commanded, and a brilliant wall of magic flew towards the native.

He shouted a strange word and crossed his arms over his chest. The magic bounced off him harmlessly.

"How do you think I survived?" he shouted, walking towards her. "There were creatures on that world that towered over me. Only by magic did I survive; only by magic have I lived a thousand years!" He pointed at her, his finger glimmering. "Kneel and pledge to follow me, little girl, and I will spare your life!"

She didn't waste breath replying. There was no one to help her, but she would never kneel, not to this murderer. "Sleep!" she shouted again, hurling magic, and then quickly again, "Sleep!"

He rocked back with the second spell, and she hoped that she had caught him off guard, but he struck with another lightning bolt that she barely deflected.

A door opened to her left, the outside door to the wine cellar. A bright golden glow came from the cellar, and she could see the bulge of the brane within. Nanny Bee held the door open.

Dear Nanny! If I can only get him close to it, if I can trick him somehow...

Nashashuk saw the door open and he pulled the tomahawk from his waist. With a cry of rage he hurled it at Nanny, and Madison could tell by the glow that he hurled it with magic behind it.

It struck Nanny in the throat, and she fell like dry sticks.

"No!" shrieked Madison. She turned and unleashed spell after spell at Nashashuk, her reason gone. Anger lent force to her magic that she had never had before, and Nashashuk was rocked back with each spell.

But there was a limit to her power, and she faltered, drained.

"Stupid child!" snarled Nashashuk, and he shot a bolt of lightning at her that she could not completely deflect. It caught her left arm and leg, and she screamed as they burned.

She fell to the ground face first and the next bolt from Nashashuk passed over her head. She looked up in anguish and saw him glaring at her triumphantly, his fingers twitching. "And now, little girl, *this* is for making me dance!"

She saw something that gave her one last cause for hope.

She raised her good hand and threw the last of her magic at him, her breath a whisper because of the pain. "No!"

He stepped back as her feeble spell hit him and he laughed. He raised his hands to cast the lethal bolt.

Two branches wrapped around him and lifted him off the ground.

Haaaaaatttte nooooiiiissssse!

Nashashuk screamed and kicked, but the tree only tightened its hold, wrapping a third branch around his legs.

"Put him in there," whispered Madison, waving her good arm at the glowing brane. She dredged a speck of magic from somewhere within her and flicked it at the tree. "Put him in there."

Yeeeesssssss.

The tree slid towards the open cellar, the grass boiling in front of it as it moved. Nashashuk shot sparks from his hands, but it only made the tree angrier. "No," he cried. "Put me down! Put me down or I'll burn you, I'll burn you like...." His voice cut off as the tree squeezed him.

Haaatte liiivviiinnnggg thiiinnngggsss!

Nashashuk shot lightning down the trunk of the tree, and the tree screamed in Madison's mind as it caught fire. It reached forward and pressed Nashashuk against the brane, and once again his body sank into the pocket universe.

The tree's branches went with him, and the tree began to be pulled into the brane also.

Noooo. Noooooooo!

The tree struggled, but inexorably the trunk was pulled in, and branch after burning branch, until the massive roots were pulled up, writhing like thick snakes as they also disappeared into the glowing brane.

The surface of the pocket universe receded, settling back into the cellar. The only sound in the night air was Madison's gasps of pain.

Through her tears she could see the crumpled form of Nanny Bee lying motionless beside the open cellar. She looked at her own arm and caught a glimpse of white bone in the black ruin of her hand. Despair and pain overcame her, and she dropped her face back into the grass.

She must have fainted, because the next thing she heard was a man's voice muttering, "Ah, young one, what an entertaining battle you fought."

Who? What?

She had never heard that voice before.

Two strong arms lifted her and cradled her. She was aware of motion, and she tried to open her eyes, but failed. She was limp as a dishrag, and her hold on her body seemed tenuous. She could hear footsteps on a wooden floor, and then feet going up the stairs. A door opened, and she sensed that she was in her own room.

"Here is your bed," the voice whispered. "Float. Float now, so you can heal and fight again. You know how to heal. Drift off to sleep, and float."

She reached down inside herself and looked for the place that lifted her up when she slept. She didn't think that she would be able to sleep, but as she tried to drift, the pain diminished, so she reached deeper and floated. The pain lessened even more, and she could tell that she was falling into unconsciousness.

"Who are you?" she whispered.

A sigh. "I don't really know. Good and evil wrapped up into a handsome prince. Something like that. Now, sleep."

She slept.

Footsteps crossed the wooden floor.

Madison heard the sound of curtains being flung open, and morning light glared through her eyelids. She plummeted to her bed as she awoke.

"Nanny?" She twisted on her bed, and looked at the silhouette in front of the window. "Is that you?"

"The early bird gets the worm, dear." Nanny Bee sat on the foot of her bed. "I'm happy to see that you lived. Does your hand hurt?"

Madison blinked her eyes, lifting her arm in front of her. The skin was puckered and discolored from her elbow to her fingertips. Pain flared when she tried to open and close her hand. "Yes. A little." She laid her hand back down on the bed. "But, but, Nanny, I saw you fall, that tomahawk caught you right in the throat!"

"Yes." She rubbed her neck, which looked flawless. "My reflexes have always been slow; I wasn't built for speed. How much did you see?" She looked at Madison, her eyes appraising.

"It looked like it cut your head clean off. I must have not seen right."

"No, you saw right." She sighed and frowned. "By the way, your arm and your leg must have been horribly burned last night for them to still look this bad in the morning."

Madison lifted her hand. "I think I saw bone showing in my hand last night. He burned my skin clear off. But, Nanny, how can you...I mean, you're still alive?"

Nanny shifted closer as though sharing a secret, and looked at Madison with clear blue eyes. "Madison, your memory renews itself the way your body does. You've forgotten, dear, that the nanomite colony inside that runs me can also repair me." She put her hand on her chest. "I am embarrassed that you saw me damaged like that. I only managed to become functional again an hour ago...."

"Nanomite colony?"

"Oh, you really have forgotten. I'm from one of the worlds that developed technology." She tapped her chest. "When this unit developed free will, I mean, when *I* developed free will, they wanted to disassemble me, but I escaped and found my way to a high mountain. The day I touched the sky, I wound up here." She put her hands in her lap. "I'm probably the last of the NanE-B models they made."

Madison reached out her good arm and rested her hand on Nanny's. "I think I remember, but only because you said it just now. You're right, my memories have faded."

"If that evil man had sent a lightning bolt at me instead of his tomahawk, I would probably be ruined. It would have burnt out....well...never mind."

She sounded embarrassed to talk about it, so Madison changed the subject. "Thank you for opening that door. You were there when I needed you."

Nanny Bee ducked her head. "I am happy to be of service. It was what I was made for, and helping you and your Uncle Roddyn is satisfying. I just don't want you to think of me as anything...odd."

"You're not odd, Nanny." Madison scooted over and hugged her with her good arm. "It's like you're the only mom I ever had, and I almost lost you. I rely on you so much and I know I never say thank you for what you do, but I am thankful."

"You're welcome."

"But Nanny, how did I get into bed?"

"I assumed you got yourself up into bed."

"No! I couldn't even move! Someone picked me up and carried me up here, and it was a man, but it wasn't Uncle Roddyn or Pinhead. I asked him who he was, and he gave an odd answer. He said he was, um, good and evil wrapped up into a handsome prince. I was too injured to even look."

Nanny shook her head. "I have no idea who that could have been. As I said, I only became functional an hour ago." She stood and brushed her pinafore apron. "Your poor Uncle Roddyn is in bad shape, though."

"Oh!" Madison put her hand to her mouth. "I forgot! How is he?"

"He's lying on his bed, with a big welt on his forehead. He barely got his shield up, but I think a falling bottle of Jack Daniels did as much damage to him as the lightning."

Madison stood up, and then cried out as her damaged leg collapsed.

Nanny held out her arm to support her. "Slowly, dear. You need another day to heal, yet." She helped Madison limp towards the stairs.

Madison was still in her party dress, now grass stained and charred. She would have slipped into jeans or sweat pants, but she was anxious to see Uncle Roddyn. "How did you get him to his bed?" she asked, as she moved down step by step.

"He was already on his bed when I got to him."

Madison stopped. "Did he wake up, then, and crawl to his bed?

"I'm afraid I was…reassembling myself at the time. I simply don't know."

Madison resumed moving down the steps. "Maybe the same person that carried me carried my uncle to his bed as well. How mysterious, like something Agatha Christie would write."

"You survived, dear, which is the important thing. I was so glad to find you floating over your bed this morning, but I am curious. What happened to Nashashuk?"

"Oh. Nashashuk backed into the tree. You know, the one that absorbed Étienne's bones? The bad tree? Nashashuk didn't know it was dangerous so he wasn't watching out for it, and it grabbed him. I persuaded the tree to put him into the brane, but then the tree got sucked in also."

"The whole tree? I am astonished." A rare smile appeared on her face. "Nashashuk must have really annoyed that tree, the way he was throwing around lightning bolts."

"It was very angry, especially after he set it on fire, but the tree didn't understand that it would get pulled in as well. It didn't want to go. The pocket universe shrank after that."

"Yes, it would. Those were two significant creatures, and they must have helped a lot to even the balance. Here he is."

Her uncle's room – the master bedroom of the tavern – was beyond the doors to the storage room and the wine cellar. Madison couldn't remember the last time she had been in this room, if she ever had. Roddyn didn't invite her into his private area.

Bookshelves lined the walls, and thick drapes were pulled aside to let in the morning light. Instruments and artifacts lay on tables in front of the bookshelves, and she recognized the Rat Witch's staff with its green gem. On the bed lay Roddyn, still in his bartender's outfit. He breathed shallowly, and high on his forehead was a large purple swelling.

"I worry," said Nanny. "I don't know what lightning does to human nervous systems."

Madison heard footsteps in the hallway, and Pinhead entered the room. "The tree is gone," he said. He saw Roddyn and stopped, rocking slowly. His finger crept up to his mouth. "Is he hurt?"

"Yes," said Madison. "But he'll get better. I think."

Nanny Bee placed Madison's good arm on the bedpost. "Wait here a moment, dear. I have an idea." She moved down the hallway.

"The bad tree is gone and won't come back," said Madison to Pinhead. She couldn't put any weight on her burnt foot; she could only use it to help steady herself.

"Good. But Roddyn is hurt."

"I know. There was a bad man here last night."

"I was asleep."

"That's okay. The bad man is gone, too."

Nanny Bee returned, carrying a box. "I suspected he had one of these in the storage room, and I was right." She lifted the lid, and there was a stethoscope sitting on top of a doctor's white coat.

Madison almost laughed. "Nanny, you're brilliant. Of course!" She pulled the stethoscope out of the box and handed it to Pinhead. "Here. Put this around your neck. No, like this. Good." She pulled out the doctor's coat. "Now slip this on."

Pinhead obediently slid his arms into the doctor's coat, and adjusted it on his shoulders.

"That's it," said Nanny Bee.

Pinhead blinked and straightened up. His eyes grew bright and focused, and he turned to Madison and took her burnt hand. "You are injured," he said, "but the cells are multiplying rapidly. There is no infection. If you were anyone else, I would send you to the hospital."

He turned to Roddyn and lifted up each of Roddyn's eyelids in turn. "This man has had a severe shock to his nervous system. Some neurons have been destroyed." He rested his thick hands on Roddyn's forehead and stared into space. "He too will recover, but he needs rest. Whether this will affect his personality is difficult to predict. His nervous system isn't the same as most humans." He winced and pressed his hand against the side of his head. "He does not heal as quickly as you do, young lady. Keep him in bed as long as he is willing." He lifted off the stethoscope and shrugged off the doctor's coat.

"Thank you, Pinhead," said Madison. Nanny folded the coat and tucked it away into the box, along with the stethoscope.

"Did I do good?" he asked, rubbing his head.

"You did good."

"I'll keep an eye on him and Uncle Roddyn," said Nanny. "You need to go back to bed, Madison. By tonight you should be able to walk."

"But...the kitchen. What about lunch?"

"The tavern will be closed today. I'll put a sign on the door and send the cook home when she arrives. Tomorrow is Sunday, and both of you can rest some more. Now go to your room. If you're hungry, I'll bring up some food."

"My chores…"

"There are only three cans of garbage. I can haul them out to the curb. Remember, the kitchen closed early last night."

With the help of Nanny Bee, Madison began hobbling back down the hallway. "Nanny, you don't know how much I appreciate you."

"Oh, I do, dear, I do. But thank you for saying it."

"And I am starving."

"I'll bring something to eat, and then you should go back to sleep."

"Yes, Nanny."

If I can sleep, knowing there is some mysterious stranger walking about who knows me. Where is he hiding?

What does he want?

Chapter Eight

The first of the two visitors came at noon, and Madison was still sleeping. She was floating and healing, so the throaty rumble of the motorcycle pulling up to the tavern mingled with her troubled dreams, as did the footsteps on the stairs.

What brought her fully awake was the gasp when somebody entered her room.

Madison opened her eyes and let herself drift down onto her bed. She turned towards the door, and there stood Penny Rusting, her hair colored an abnormal red, her scarf half unwound, her mouth open. "Hello," said Madison, which didn't quite seem adequate.

"Uh..." Penny closed her mouth and swallowed.

Madison pushed herself up so that she was sitting. Before her nap, she had discarded the ruined party dress and put on shorts and a t-shirt that read, "They laughed when I said I'd be a comedian. They're not laughing now!"

She could tell by Penny's reaction that she must have seen her floating above the bed. "I'm sorry I can't get up," she said, pretending that everything was normal. She held out her left arm, which was still darkly discolored. "There was a fight last night, and I got hurt."

Penny's mothering instincts must have moved her off of dead center, because she made an Oh with her mouth when she saw Madison's arm. "Maddy..."

"Yes?"

67

"Are you possessed?"

Madison laughed, louder than was polite. With all the chaos she had gone through, Penny thinking that her floating was because of some demon possession struck her as funny. "No, heavens, no. You mean because I was above my bed just now?"

Penny nodded, her face concerned. "That's not normal, you know."

Madison sighed.

How to explain it?

I've always been taught never to tell the real truth. But is there any explanation that would be more easily believed than the truth?

"I'm a bit of a special child, I'm afraid." She ran her fingers back and forth on her coverlet, a secondhand Amish quilt with hex shapes sewn into it. "I have some magic inside me. Seriously. I was born with it. And when I'm sleeping, especially when I'm hurt, I can float a little so I heal better. I know nobody else does that, but other than that, I'm just a normal girl."

Sort of.

Penny sat at the foot of Madison's bed, her brow furrowed. "Can you....fly?"

Madison laughed again. "No. I wish I could. That would be fun. And I can't jump over buildings or bend steel or see through things. But I do make good soup."

"Yes, you do." Penny's forehead relaxed and the mood eased slightly. "I saw the tavern was closed, but I left my phone behind in a booth last night and I wanted to get it. No one was around and I saw your room was open. I didn't mean to be nosey. Is Roddyn ok? You said there was a fight."

Madison lost her smile. Again, she had to be delicate about how much to tell. "It happened when we locked up. One of the patrons was, um, drunk and when Roddyn tried to get him to leave, it turned into a fight."

"What happened to you? How did you get hurt?"

Why would I have been in the fight? And what should I say happened to my arm...a burn, a scald...was I cleaning up? Was there a fire?

I'm taking too long to answer.

Penny folded her arms. "You're not being honest with me, are you?" It wasn't a question.

"Not, um, completely."

"Listen, Madison, I've seen some strange things in my life. Never anyone floating above their bed, mind you, but strange things, like that ghost in your back yard, for instance. You're not telling me everything because you're afraid I won't believe you. Or is it because you're afraid I *will* believe you?"

"I..." She shook her head, and exhaled. Her arm hurt and her leg hurt, and she was too worn out to make up any more stories. "The man we fought with could throw lightning. I got burnt, and Uncle Roddyn got, I guess you could say, shocked. And he hit his head, and he's still unconscious."

Penny nodded slowly, digesting Madison's statements. "The man could throw lightning." She stood up and looked out the back window, her hands resting on the sill. "This place fascinates me, you know that? I feel drawn to it. It's like, it's a little enclave that hasn't caught up to the modern day yet." She rubbed the eagle on her arm. "That ghost we saw. What was his name?"

"I forgot you saw the ghost. His name was Étienne. He hasn't come back."

"I do believe in some crazy stuff. Crystals, mesmerism, feng shui. Did you know that this tavern is actually oriented right to receive positive *qi?* I love it here." She turned from the window. "Don't worry, Maddy. I don't think you're possessed, not with an evil spirit, anyway. You're not supposed to talk about this to other people?"

Madison shook her head slowly, her face solemn.

"Then I'll live by the same rule. I won't even mention it to Roddyn. Will you tell him I hope he gets well soon? I'll be back to check up. Okay?"

"Sure. That would be nice." She ventured a smile. "Thank you for understanding."

"I'll go find my phone and then let myself out. You go back to resting." She stepped closer and touched Madison's burned hand, her fingers tentative on the discolored flesh. "That must have been some fight."

"It was. But we won."

"I should hope. You rest. I'll see you later." She patted Madison on the head, which was annoying, but she endured it because Penny meant well.

"Okay. Bye." Madison watched her go down the stairs.

That could have turned out worse.

She lay back on the bed, and elevated. It seemed easier than before. It used to be a reflex that happened only after she fell asleep. Maybe if she could control it better, she really could fly.

Too many things are happening, and this could get out of control. I guess Penny will tell Mitch – maybe not – and then word could spread. This place could become a madhouse if it isn't kept quiet.

I wonder if I can bend steel bars?

"Nah." She closed her eyes.

The room felt wrong.

Madison came fully awake and lowered herself onto her bed. It was past noon, judging by the direction of the sun, which no longer shone into her window. She had no clock – the electric motor thing – so she always relied on Nanny Bee's sense of time. Downstairs, an old Big Ben clock run by counterweights kept the hours.

What's wrong with my room?

She stood up and balanced on her good leg. Carefully she scanned the room, looking for anything out of place. Her vanity and mirror were straight; the mess from last night when she tried to make herself up was gone, the work of Nanny Bee. Riviere's painting of Saint George slaying the dragon was in its usual place, as well as Vermeer's Milkmaid over her headboard. On either side hung shelves of books, old classics and fairy tales.

She hobbled to her closet, and peered inside. It was a generous closet, considering the age of the tavern, but there was no one there.

Under the bed? Don't be silly.

She lowered herself down to peer under the bed. It was spotless, of course, with a couple of boxes of stored winter clothes and nothing else.

Empty. I must be imagining things.

She struggled back to her feet, lay down, and elevated herself again. She didn't feel sleepy, but she knew her body needed healing.

She had no idea why the room felt wrong, but it still did, in spite of her searching. Either something was missing, or something was there that shouldn't be.

Whatever it was, it would have to wait.

She slept fitfully for another hour. When she awoke, the room felt normal again.

She managed to get through the rest of Saturday without incident. She finished the *No. 1 Lady's Detective Agency* as she floated and made a mental note to ask Mrs. Regan to get some of the sequels on the next library run. She ate ravenously. Her body was healing itself, and the supply of sliced meats diminished rapidly as Nanny Bee kept her supplied with sandwiches.

Uncle Roddyn woke up in the afternoon, groggy and confused. Nanny tended him, bringing food and drink, but he wasn't hungry. Madison hobbled down the steps to visit him, and he asked twice what had happened to Nashashuk, but seemed not to be able to keep it in his head. Pinhead said that Roddyn would heal slowly.

Sunday morning Madison woke up with some strength in her hand and leg and only a little discoloration to show that she had been injured. She diced a tomato and some ham, sautéed a bit of chopped onion, and made an omelet for herself and Roddyn. Roddyn ate a little, asked again about Nashashuk, and went back to sleep.

Obviously, there wouldn't be a Grand Homework Review today.

Madison was disappointed. She worked diligently on her studies every day – well, almost every day, unless there was a Vernal Equinox party and some stupid guy named Corey was expected to show up.

She was quite done with Emily Dickinson, but she still had her geology text to study. There was a chapter on fossil fuels and how they formed, and another on precious minerals. The text had lots of photos, and she studied them carefully.

She went outside and sat in the sun, enjoying the birds and the warm spring breeze with the fragrance of blossoms, and thought how grateful she was not to have allergies. She was also grateful not to see any Escaped cavorting around.

After a while she got up and walked around to the back of the tavern, pleased to have two good legs again, though she was not up to running. She went out to the shed, chatted with Nanny Bee who was folding aprons, and grabbed a chocolate ice cream bar out of the freezer. She finished it by the time she was back inside the tavern, tossed the stick into the garbage, grabbed another detective novel – *The Big Sleep* – and went back up to her room. Inside the door she stopped dead still.

It felt wrong again.

Someone or something was there. She could feel it, even though every corner of her room was clearly empty.

She frowned, her temper rising. There was something very annoying about the whole situation.

It was time to take action.

She stood in the arch of the doorway and rubbed her fingers together until her hands were rich with magic, and then she cast it into the room and commanded, "Show yourself!" The room flashed with brilliant light.

"Argh!"

In the corner of the room, between her bed and the painting of Saint George, a figure flashed into view. Madison put up her hands defensively; she had learned how to cast a shield, and she was ready.

The person in the corner surprised her, though. He had a shining black pageboy haircut and a gold circlet around his head. He wore a red cape over his shoulders, a gold-embroidered blue tunic on his torso, and a pair of brown tights. From his thick leather belt hung an ornate sword. He was handsome to the point of being a caricature, with a dimple on his chin.

"All right, who are you?" said Madison firmly. She might be only fourteen, but she wasn't going to put up with someone skulking around in her room.

The person winced. "Damon."

"What are you doing in my room?"

"Observing. Learning. Keeping out of sight and not bothering anyone."

She flexed her fingers. Another Escaped, and maybe she was healed enough to cope with it. She had to be. Uncle Roddyn was still in bed, recovering. "Why in my room?"

"Because you're the interesting one."

"What do you mean?"

He laughed. "This place is littered with the mundane and the bizarre, but you are hard to figure out. Besides, it was a young virgin like you that got me into this mess."

She narrowed her eyes. His phrases were a bit odd, and she didn't know if she liked being labeled a young virgin. It was true, but not polite. Also, he used English oddly, like a mixture of the modern and the archaic. "What world are you from?"

He pursed his lips and nodded. "Very astute. You're right. I'm not from around here." He glanced at the walls of the room as though surveying Madison's world. "No, it's quite different than where I came from." His eyes snapped back to her. "My world is called Beleyenth, although I don't know what good it does you to know that. If you'll stand aside, I'll go amuse myself elsewhere."

She heard footsteps coming up the stairs behind her. She determined to keep the Escaped named Damon in her room a moment more.

"You've been in my room before, right?"

"Yes, many times. As I said, you're the only interesting person here."

I might have been changing clothes some of those times. I really don't like this person.

Madison walked to the foot of her bed, and Nanny Bee stepped in to the room. She was carrying Roddyn's double-barreled shotgun, which she aimed at Damon. "I saw the flash in your room," Nanny said, "and decided you might need some help."

"Oh, perfect," said Damon, rolling his eyes. "The wind-up toy arrives carrying a shotgun. That won't do you any good; in fact, you could seriously mess up the paintings."

"Just stay where you are," said Nanny.

"Let me show you something." Damon pulled a thin black dagger with a golden handle from his waist.

Nanny raised the shotgun in warning, and Madison began rubbing her fingers together.

Damon sighed. "If it will make you feel better, shoot me now and repair the wall later, but I'm just going to stand here. Now watch." He lifted his hand and sliced his index finger with the sharp point of the dagger. Madison gasped.

74

A thin dark smoke emerged from the wound, flowed out an inch and writhed for a moment. Then it flowed back into his finger and the cut closed up.

Damon slid the knife into the sheath on his belt, and then snapped the fingers on the hand he had just cut. "All better. You see? So why don't you lower your useless shotgun, you fancy clockwork lady, and let us act civilized."

"What was that?" asked Madison. "What was that darkness in your finger?"

Damon grinned, his black eyes crinkling. "Pure evil. The absolute essence of evil. I kid you not, as they say."

"I don't believe it. How did you get this way?"

His grin disappeared. "You want a story. You want to know about me. How touching. But I hope now you understand that a shotgun blast will do nothing to me, and that your magic, though it pulled me from hiding, cannot interfere with me."

Impulsively, Madison snapped her hands out and commanded, "Sleep!"

The wave of magic engulfed Damon, passed through him, and dissipated on the wall behind. The painting of the milkmaid tilted slightly.

Damon snarled and pointed his finger at her in return. "Die!" he commanded, and a black wave flew across the room. Before she could duck, it washed over her and faded away, leaving the room smelling sour. She was unharmed.

Damon laughed loud and long. "Oh, the expression on your face! That was beyond price. You actually were frightened. And look." He pointed to Nanny with a satisfied smirk. "The tick-tock lady was smart enough not to bother shooting at me. You are a clever unit, indeed."

"That wasn't funny," snapped Madison.

"Yes, it *was* funny," said Damon, just as forcefully. "Not only have you learned that you can't harm me, but also, apparently, I can't harm you, although on my world that spell would have killed a whole crowd of peasants. I shouldn't have let you know that, I suppose. Now you'll impose on me, ask me to entertain you, to dance the Twist with you or some such abomination."

"How long have you been here?"

"Again, the request for a story."

Madison's temper was short. "Tell me!"

Damon jerked at her shouted command. "I came into your world six days ago! Do you need to know the hour and the minute?"

"No."

She counted back. That would make it three days before she saw the Rat Witch. Uncle Roddyn had returned an Escaped, a thin person in a green robe, back to his brane probably the day after Damon had arrived.

Something has changed, Pinhead said. Could it be this obnoxious creature?

"Where have you been since you got here?"

"Oh, here and there. Keeping hidden." He straightened the painting of the milkmaid. "Learning. This world is different than the one I came from. Magic works differently there. *I* was different there."

"And my sleep spell won't affect you? It usually does work, you know."

"If I were flesh and blood, I suppose it might have put me out. I used to be flesh and blood. We would have had a great fight, you and I, if you had met me in my earlier years. I wasn't as nice then, I assure you."

"This is you being nice?"

Damon smiled, a cruel smile that looked vile on the face of a handsome prince. "Yes, Madison. This is me being nice. I hope it won't last much longer."

"I would hate to know you when you weren't being nice."

His face grew cold. "You wouldn't have known me for long."

Oh, how I wish Uncle Roddyn were here. Damon's as bad as Nashashuk and much, much worse than the Rat Witch.

"I can help you get back to your own world," she said.

He pushed out his lower lip. "I don't want to go back to my world. They want me dead. In fact, they killed me once already."

Madison's leg began to pain her again. She had been on her feet too long. "Will you at least go downstairs so we can sit?"

And maybe Uncle Roddyn will wake up in his right mind and help me get rid of this creature.

Damon looked at his nails – uselessly, because like the rest of his appearance, they were perfect – and nodded. Nanny Bee carried the useless shotgun downstairs and stowed it behind the bar, and Madison and Damon sat down near Emtianal.

Emtianal's avatar activated, straightened up, and opened its eyes.

"Hello, there, moth-man," said Damon.

Emtianal raised his eyebrows and looked at Madison questioningly.

"We found him in my room," said Madison.

"Yes," said Damon, "in a corner like a dust mop. If I hadn't been discovered, Miss Crankshaft here might have used me to sweep under the bed."

"I started sensing him now and then," explained Madison. "He's been all over the place, I guess."

Damon smiled. "Upstairs, downstairs, and in my lady's chamber."

"If you're from another world, how do you know about shotguns?"

"Your Uncle Roddyn aimed that thing at the madman, what was his name, Nashashuk? So I looked at it while everyone else was sleeping. It's easy to figure out, if you are smarter than a herdsman."

"How did you learn to speak English? No one cast a Common Tongue spell on you."

"How do you know that *you're* speaking English? Maybe you're speaking my language and don't know it. I could have cast a Common Tongue spell on you while you slept, you know."

Madison put her fingers to her lips and frowned.

That's a pretty puzzle. How would I know I were speaking a foreign tongue, if I understood it like my own? I guess I would think it was my own language if the words had the same meaning.

The clue is in the words, not the meaning. What is it where the words are as important as the meaning?

She brightened and put her hand down. "'High in the pine tree, the little turtledove, made a little nursery, to please her little love.' There, that rhymed! When a poem is translated to another language, it doesn't rhyme in that language unless you alter the lines! I didn't change it a bit and it still rhymed. So I *am* speaking English and so are you." She smiled smugly.

Nanny murmured, "And you thought studying poetry was useless."

Damon rubbed his chin, a bemused smile on his overly handsome face. "Well done, little girl. Well done, indeed. You see? You *are* the interesting one here." He turned to Nanny. "However, you, you mechanical servant, you and I have much more in common. Neither of us has a heart, and neither of us can hoist a tankard and drink it down. We are the hollow people, you and I."

"I am not hollow," said Nanny.

Damon ignored her remark as he cast an envious glance towards the bar. "Here we sit in a tavern and I cannot drink. I would give anything for a cold refreshment, even for a bottle of that child's drink you sell, that *root beer*."

"Why can't you drink?" asked Madison.

He opened his mouth and pointed to the darkness inside. "It's got no place to go. I'm not thirsty, in the sense that I need water, and yet I am."

"Did you carry me to my room after I got hurt?"

"Oh, that. Well, yes, I did. It just seemed a waste to let you lie there and die. I dragged that bartender to his bed also. Then I swept the tavern and did the laundry."

"Liar," said Nanny.

78

"Of course."

"So," asked Madison, "why do you speak English?"

"Our worlds are uniquely close, it seems. Not only do we wander into your universe, but some of your people and creatures wander into mine. Particularly those awful things you call *crows* and *snakes*. Just when we think they are only creatures of legend, one of them enters our world and terrorizes everyone again." He cleared his throat.

He has no throat. That's just a mannerism, a habit of when he was flesh and blood.

Damon continued, "Our languages and our stories influence each other. What I've learned since crossing over is that you speak a variant of one of our languages. Being rather brilliant, I have adapted my speech to yours. I've also seen stories in your books that you call fairy tales that are actual tales from our own history, and we have fables that, it turns out, are parts of your own history."

"That's interesting, but I want to learn about you," said Madison. "Tell me your story."

Damon winced. "Yes, I will, but first will you please stop issuing Commands? You are not a princess."

"What do you mean, Commands?"

"Orders. Demands." He banged his fist on the table. "It's a bit of magic you are obviously unfamiliar with but is still in effect for me. Very well. I will tell you my story. But I warn you, it is not fit for young ladies, it is not uplifting, and if you have nightmares in the middle of the night, don't say I didn't warn you!"

Chapter Nine

Damon stretched his legs out and put his boots on a chair. He leaned back against the dark red cushion of the booth and his eyes focused on some point in the distance.

"My story. She Commands me to tell my story. Very well. I started out decently enough, others might say. My parents were wealthy – my father traded jewelry – and my mother and I were very close. She read to me, taught me, we would go boating together, she saw to it that I was churched, but when I was ten, she took sick and died. I found out that she had been poisoned by my Father. You gasp at that? Then think of what it did to me. Think of how that wrenched my soul when my faithless father had become enamored of a woman of wealth, and she had encouraged him to kill my mother.

"I hated them both, my father and my stepmother. They had destroyed the center of my existence, the wellspring of my life, for their own selfish desires. They hated me in turn, as I was a living reminder of their sins. My father considered me worthless baggage, so he sent me to an academy in a far country. I'm surprised they didn't poison me also.

"The academy was useless, a place for children of the wealthy to be stabled and poorly taught, but while there I encountered a sorcerer who began teaching me the dark arts. I determined to live up to my father's low opinion of me, so I shed all the values I had been taught. After all, what had these values gotten me but sorrow and despair, while my father and stepmother lived a life of luxury? I began learning all the banned and evil knowledge of the ages. My teacher pretended to be an academy historian, but for me he was a fountain of forbidden knowledge.

"A cousin wrote me that my new stepmother had begun drinking and spending her wealth foolishly, and I was pleased. When I was informed that my stepmother had died in the streets and that my father had disappeared to escape his debts, I rejoiced! It didn't matter that I was ejected from the academy for poverty. By then I knew the way to power and wealth. I killed my teacher, and took over his holdings."

He looked at Madison. "Your mouth is open. It makes you look dull-witted."

She closed her mouth with an audible snap.

He shrugged. "Don't be surprised at my actions. After all, my teacher had killed his own teacher to obtain his position. To me, life was no longer precious. I was just a creature of nature trying to survive.

"To shorten the story, I became powerful and insidious. With my skills, I found that there was no office that I could not influence, no king that I could not sway, no magistrate that I could not buy, and no woman that I could not corrupt.

"Treasure was not enough. I took to satisfying my desires for power, destroying lives for the pleasure of it, just as my mother's happy life had been destroyed. I looked for happy, peaceful citizens and by subtle means brought them down. By day I walked the city streets, a kind man with gold threads in my cloak and pupils by my side, and everyone bowed to the wise and beneficent Damon. I healed many children that I had sickened by night, I gave comfort to those suffering from disasters that I had brought upon them, and where I passed, the beggars rejoiced because of my coins, not knowing that I was the cause of their poverty.

"Eventually, I was found out.

"There were perceptive people, people who used magic for good, who discerned the webs that ensnared the city, and the webs all led to me. They whispered, they plotted, and I was too sated with my success and sotted with my own power to beware of treachery.

"They came at me before dawn, with torches and, yes, even pitchforks. In the forefront were those clerics and thaumaturgies and dowagers that could protect the rest from my spells. At first I thought that I and a couple of my devoted pupils could run or hide." He winked at Madison. "I am very good at hiding."

"No, you're not."

He frowned. "I was. But the dowagers discerned me, and the clerics combined their spells, and I was hounded – literally – to the outskirts of the city, and then to a bluff overlooking the Gladwyne River. I turned and hurled a spell of death at them – as I did at you – and any one of them alone would have died instantly, but together they resisted me. Then the glimmer of dawn came, and as is the nature of dark magic, I weakened. My back was to the river, and they had me circled on all sides.

"They combined their magic and cast a spell of Banishment on me, a spell that threw me into a state between life and death. I did not suspect that these supposedly 'good' people could cast such a spell, but I was overcome. I froze, and I toppled towards the river.

"One of my pupils, thinking to do me a favor, modified the Banishment as I fell."

Madison furrowed her brow. "Modified?"

"He added an addendum, a codicil, an amendment; it was a group spell that took me down, and therefore was subject to being modified, whereas a spell from a single caster could not. Is that clear now? A nod would be sufficient. Thank you.

"'Til the sun shines on you again,' he said, and I believe they beat him to death for it. I know I would have killed him had I had the chance. An old weather witch, who understood his addendum, called down a storm, a deluge, a flood that raged many days. When the waters receded, the Gladwyne had changed its course, and my body was caught in the roots of a young hawthorn tree, buried under flood soil.

"Generations passed. I was not alive, but I was not dead either, though I would have preferred it. Can you imagine endless time, buried, encased in darkness, and yet still able to reason? I felt no guilt for my crimes; instead I felt unjustly condemned, misunderstood and mistreated. I seethed and raged. I wove endless plans of vengeance until I grew black with desire. I was a murderer without remorse and I had given up everything from my youth that might have given me peace. Even the memory of my mother was reduced to her last moments of agony caused by my father's poison. I lived upon mental bile and spiritual gall."

He dropped his feet to the floor and looked at Madison, his eyes challenging. "Are you sure you want to hear this? I know some good fairy tales. Hardly any death at all."

"Go on," said Madison. She was intrigued. It seemed an awful fate, and yet not less than Damon deserved.

He shrugged and stretched out his legs again. "Very well, where was I? Oh, yes. About six feet under. I decayed. I dwindled. My physical body dissipated, and the hawthorn tree absorbed much of my nature."

He glanced at Madison. "Ever meet a tree with issues?" Again, he winked. "Then you know what I mean. If I could have been aware of what transpired above me, I'm sure I would have seen foul murders and lovers' trysts gone awry beneath its branches, but I had nothing to amuse me, nothing. How many years passed? I really don't know.

"Eventually the Gladwyne eroded its way back to the hawthorn tree, now twisted with age, and a bank swallow's nest gave way. I was exposed; a ray of sun shone upon my back and finally I was free of the Banishment, free to move, and yet I dared not. The full sun, after all these ages of darkness, would have destroyed me, would have burned me to dust and true death.

"I waited until midnight, more impatient than through all the centuries of my burial, and then flowed out, a pool of blackness in the night, a black fog creeping over the ground. I needed a sleeping person, someone helpless that I could enter and possess.

"By chance I found a brick wall, and a garden, a palace garden. I was thoroughly mad, I'm sure, and desperate to live and breathe again, and then to wrack this land to its very marrow.

"I flowed into a bedroom and rose up, a black wraith. There, upon the bed, lay a young girl, younger than you." He dipped his head at Madison. "How excellent, I gibbered, excellent, because once I have taken over the body of this lovely innocent I shall corrupt and destroy in a manner that has never been seen in all this world.

"Then she woke up.

"'Who are you?' she asked, as though I was one of her servants.

"'I am one risen from the grave,' I whispered, 'and I have come to…'

"'Oh, never mind,' she said, with the air of one used to interrupting. 'I'm thirsty.'

"'Thirsty? Yes, soon we will slake our thirst upon the blood of…'

"'Get me a drink of water,' she said, or rather, Commanded. In my world," he shifted in his seat, "in my world, the ancient magic of an innocent virgin, no matter how spoiled and self-centered, is extremely powerful, especially against pure evil." He spread his hands as he explained. "Most people are a mix of good and evil, so an innocent virgin's Commands are mild in nature and can be resisted, but against pure evil – me – the Command was absolute."

He put his hands together. "Water. She wanted water. I had no choice. But before I could act, she made it worse. 'And make it cold and clean,' she insisted. A lesser sorcerer would have dissipated in failure, but I was able to conjure a crystal goblet of pure cold water and a physical hand to reach it to her. I promised myself at that moment, that when I possessed her, I would keep her soul as a choice nugget to chew over on quiet evenings when I was in my power."

Madison shivered. She began to comprehend what Damon meant when he said his essence was pure evil.

"She drank noisily, set it on her night stand, and Commanded, 'Tell me a story.'

"A story. I thought of all my deeds past, and chuckled. I'm afraid it sounded like rotten trees snapping. 'I can tell you stories of such horror and despair that your blood would curdle and your spleen....'

"'No, no, no. One of the nice stories so I can go to sleep. Tell me the story of Goldenhair and the three *Borogars*.'

"She Commanded me, but I did not know the deeds of Goldenhair and his battles with the three *Borogars*. All this time, you see, I am standing in the dark, and she is not looking closely at me, because who pays attention to a servant? 'I do not know that story,' I am forced to say."

"'Okay, then tell me the story of Snow White.'

"I had been buried too many centuries. 'I know him not,' I said. If she had stopped issuing Commands, if she had only been quiet for a moment, I could have gathered myself and possessed her, but no, she spoke again.

"'Her. Snow White's a her. Okay, it's like this. It goes like this. I'm Snow White, okay? The Wicked Queen is jealous because I'm so beautiful so she gave me a poisoned fruit and I'm lying here dead.'

"That sounded like a wonderful story to me, a marvelous story. Jealousy, poison, death, what redeeming features in a fairy tale!

"'Then the handsome prince comes and wakes her up.' And she issued the worst Command of all, 'You have to be the Handsome Prince.'

"'What?' I said, horrified. My form wavered and writhed.

"'You know. Able to slay dragons, good and kind and noble and stuff like that,' she said. 'You have to be the Handsome Prince.'"

Madison smiled. She could see the trap that Damon would have been in.

"You would not smile," said Damon, "if you knew my pain. I had no choice; my form altered, my essence changed, all the fibers of my being conformed to the young girl's command.

"'Now,' she said, lying back on the pillow, 'I am Sleeping Beauty and you must kiss me awake.'

"Now is when I would have possessed her and rent her soul, but now I could not. It was impossible. I had changed. Instead, I stepped out of the shadows and kissed her on the forehead. She opened her eyes and gasped when she saw me. 'Who are you?' she asked, sitting bolt upright.

"I looked at myself in the mirror, and I was the way you see me now, though my eyes were blue and I had a beating heart. 'I am your Handsome Prince, as you Commanded. My name is Damon, and I have come to save you from the poisoned apple, and now you must be my bride.'

"'But, but, that was only a fairy tale,' she said, 'and I'm only ten years old!'

"'Then,' I said, 'I will go out into the world and seek my fortune, and when you turn eighteen I will return and take you to where I am hailed as a true prince, and you will be my bride, and we will live happily ever after.' Can you believe I said such tripe?" Damon made a sour face and wiped his mouth with the back of his hand.

"'That...that would be nice,' she said. She put her head back on the pillow and mumbled, 'I must be dreaming.'

"I left her as she slept. I vaulted over the windowsill into the garden, and went out into the world a changed creature. Unfortunately, the rest of the world was not a fairy tale. Luck did not smile upon me, and I never did gather a fortune. I was noble and good, but as I had learned from my childhood, there was not much profit in it. Finally I sought the mountains, hoping to find gold or other such riches before the young lady became married to another suitor."

Damon stood up and brushed off his tunic, as though brushing off memories. "One day I touched the sky, as they all say, and my story ends. The trouble is, this world of yours has different rules, and the magic of the pocket universe extends only so far.

"I am no longer noble and good. Since leaving my world, my insides have become unwoven and lost their purity, but my outer form remains. I seem to be good on the outside and evil on the inside, and I have blood on my hands. I'm not sure what I am." He exhaled as though reliving his past had tired him. "So, Miss Madison, would you be so kind as to not issue Commands right and left? I find you resistible, but only with effort."

"We need to return you to your world," said Madison. "You're throwing the universes out of balance."

"There's no hurry in that regard. Getting that irritable oak tree as well as Nashashuk back into the pocket universe evened things a bit, as I heard you explain. Besides, you can Command me all you want and I will resist because I am now a mix of good and evil, so it's not something that you can order me to do. No, you'll have to trick me in some way, and I'll be watching for it. Besides, I like it here. In this world, I don't have to live up to that imperative, that Command, to be good. I find being good a waste."

Madison heard a couple of motorcycles pull up to the front. Mitch and Penny must be back to visit. "Why? Why is it a waste to be good?"

"There's no profit in it. It became obvious to me after all those years I spent seeking my fortune. For example, if I had given my gold to the poor, then I also would have become poor. But if I had stolen a silver candlestick from a church, then I would have been wealthy. Evil is profitable, and what you call goodness is not. Simple logic says that good people wind up poor and bad people wind up prosperous. I prefer prosperous." He smiled.

"You're wrong, Damon." Madison got to her feet to answer the knock. "I don't have an answer at the tip of my tongue, but you're wrong and I know it." She went to the tavern's front door, and let in Mitch and Penny.

They entered with smiles and chatter and a paper plate heavy with brownies. Madison took one and shared them with Mitch and Penny, and then she jabbered away about nothing as she covered the rest and set them on the counter. Neither Emtianal, nor Nanny Bee, nor Damon could eat a brownie. Emtianal only drank milk and other liquids, Nanny Bee plugged herself in at night in her closet – she was from the pocket universe and didn't have problems with electricity the way hair driers did – and Damon, well, Damon seemed to have a magical existence and couldn't eat or drink if he wanted to. Only Uncle Roddyn and Pinhead could help her enjoy the brownies.

Penny noticed Damon standing behind Madison. "Hi, I'm Penny. What are you dressed up for?" she asked as a way of making conversation.

"I'm not dressed up for anything," said Damon, his hand on his ornate sword. He stared at Penny's unnaturally red hair and asked, "Is that hair from a clown outfit?"

Penny's smile froze, and Madison quickly spoke up. "Don't mind Damon. He's one of our, ah, unusual guests."

"Oh, I see," said Penny, her voice touched with frost.

"That's right," said Damon with a manic smile, "just one more inmate of The Padded Cell!"

Mitch stuck out his hand. "My name's Mitch."

"And my name is Damon. You're a brave man, Mitch." They shook hands, to Madison's surprise, and Mitch didn't ask why Damon thought he was brave, which Madison thought was wise.

Penny turned her attention back to Madison. "So, how is Uncle Roddyn doing?"

Roddyn spoke up as he entered slowly from his room, surprising them. "Doing okay, I guess, thanks for asking." He

88

helped himself to a brownie. "Penny, Mitch, thanks for stopping by. Madison, who's your guest?"

"I didn't know you were up," she said, hurrying to his side. She helped him onto a stool, and brought him a glass of milk from the kitchen. "Uncle, this is Damon."

"So I heard. When did he turn up?"

Damon made a mock bow. "I've been around for a few days, Mister Roddyn. I simply prefer not to be noticed."

Madison put her hand on her uncle's shoulder. "How are you feeling now?"

"Not good. Nice brownies, though. Penny, you make these yourself?"

"From a box mix, but they've got chocolate chunks in them, so they're my favorite."

"I don't think I can open the tavern tomorrow," said Roddyn. "I know tomorrow's Monday, but I can hardly walk, and I don't have any ambition. All I want to do is sleep."

Mitch and Penny looked at each other, and then Mitch said, "We were talking about that. Listen, we helped out during the Vernal Equinox. We're used to working with your customers. What if we were to close our shop for a week and come help out? It's slow right now, we like working here, and it would be fun."

"Huh." Roddyn stared past them, thinking. "Yeah, I suppose so. I can't pay you much."

He could be a lot more grateful. And we're not short on money.

Madison kept silent, but she didn't like the way Uncle Roddyn was acting. His gentleness was gone. Nanny Bee sat down by Emtianal and listened. Damon got bored and walked away, then disappeared, literally.

"Can we keep our tips?" asked Penny.

"Oh, sure, sure," said Roddyn. "No problem."

"Then I think we'll make out okay. You'll have to show me how to work that hand-cranked cash register, though, if you're not behind the bar to run it. Ours at the bike shop is computerized."

"Madison can do it. She knows everything here."

"You open in the morning at ten," said Penny. "Should we come at nine?"

"Nine-thirty," said Roddyn. "Listen, Madison can answer any questions. I'm sorry; I've got to lie down again." He slid off the bar stool, and Nanny Bee was there to support him and help him back to bed.

"Poor Roddyn," said Penny. "He looks, I don't know, almost defeated."

"He's just tired," said Madison. "I'm sure he's really grateful you guys will be here. Let me show you how to work the cash register." She pointed out that they started with fifty dollars in change at the start, and that they should keep the paper receipts the machine cranked out. Mitch already understood that they didn't take credit cards – the sign by the register said CASH OR CHECKS ONLY. The regulars knew to pay cash, and the occasional traveler who only had plastic was told to pay the next time they came by. Most of them did.

Madison grabbed another brownie off of the tray, grateful that weight gain was never a concern for her. "Oh, and don't worry about Emtianal. You can just ignore him when you close up."

"He never gets up? He never moves?" whispered Penny.

"No." Madison looked at Mitch. "Mr. McKenzie, you do understand that this place is different? Right?"

"You can call me Mitch, and remember, I did see that ghost."

"Well, you might see more than that, but I hope not. Anyway, Emtianal is special, and Nanny can take care of him. But if you do see someone or something strange, be sure to tell me, unless Uncle Roddyn is up and around. Oh, and if your motorcycles won't start? Let me know and I'll make them start."

"Why do you say our motorcycles won't start?"

"Uncle Roddyn tells people the story that it's because of a concentration of lodestone under the tavern, so we can't have TVs and stuff like that. People accept that. The real reason, though, is

90

that motors in general don't work close to the tavern, and you've been parking your bikes up on the concrete near the door. That's why the parking lot is so far away, so the cars can start. The further away from the tavern you get, the more normal things are."

"I got my motor started yesterday after I found my phone," said Penny, "but it didn't want to. I had to cuss at it before it would start. I hoped you couldn't hear."

"Whatever works."

Some people, like Nashashuk, learn to channel the magic even though they're from this world. I wonder if Penny has that skill? That could be useful, if they keep helping at the bar.

"Madison," asked Mitch, "Penny didn't tell me much about that fight. Roddyn's got a goose egg on his forehead. How did that happen?"

"Someone didn't want to leave the Equinox party, and Uncle Roddyn got hit by a whiskey bottle. But that's all over; you shouldn't worry about it. Things are usually so quiet here that it's boring. You won't see any fights." She put the last of her brownie in her mouth.

"Penny also said that you can fly."

Madison choked.

"I did not say that!" said Penny, swatting him on the shoulder. "You never listen to me! I said that she could float over her bed."

"I can't fly," said Madison, after swallowing. "But Penny was right, I float when I sleep. This place has magic in it, but we don't want people to know. I'm afraid that part of your job, Mr....um, I mean, Mitch, Penny, is for you to make the place seem normal to everyone. The regulars understand that this place can be odd at times, and so we try to make it seem like we're deliberately being old-fashioned."

"I think I'm going to enjoy this." Penny walked the length of the counter and picked up a rag. "This could be fun."

"It should be." Madison sat down on a bar stool and watched the two bikers checking out the supplies behind the bar.

"Seriously, things have really settled down since that fight. I don't think anything unusual will happen while you're helping out."

She couldn't have been more wrong.

Chapter Ten

Monday morning.

She looked at the back yard through her broken window, grateful that it wasn't raining. Today they could get a workman out to fix the damage. There was no longer a tree outside her window, so she would have to invent some story about throwing a Frisbee too high or something to explain the damage.

Her arms and legs were perfectly strong and whole today, so she did her chores, hauling the garbage cans down the entrance road to the highway. Nanny was watching her, probably checking to see if she was healthy, so she ran back from the highway at a full run and did a victory lap around Nanny.

Then she stopped. "Nanny, I have a question."

"Yes, dear?"

"That rat witch made some of the fruit ripe – see those cherries there? – she made them suddenly become ripe, even though they were just blossoms. Should we harvest them? Are they safe to eat?"

"Let me check." They walked over to the odd branch, heavy with dark ripe bing cherries, while the other branches were still shedding petals from their blossoms.

Nanny plucked one of the low-hanging cherries and placed it in her mouth. Her eyes got a faraway look, and Madison had to resist the urge to listen to Nanny's chest to see if she could hear the sounds of the cherry being analyzed.

Nanny nodded. "They are perfectly normal. You might ask Pinhead to harvest them, and those apricots also. The rat witch seems only to have shifted the seasons for these fruit, not changed them into anything unnatural."

"Uncle Roddyn said he was going to try to figure out her staff. That would be cool to have fresh cherries anytime we wanted."

"I think not. Changing the flow of time could have consequences. Just because we escaped disaster this time doesn't mean we'll always be so lucky."

"Maybe, but it would still be cool."

She ran into the tavern and found Pinhead, who had on a straw hat and was getting ready to work in the herb garden. He nodded and said "Okay" when she asked him to harvest the fruit on the tree. Then she ran upstairs to shower and change out of her garbage clothes. Today she felt like running everywhere with her healthy legs and arms.

She paused before taking off her work clothes and frowned. Where was Damon? "Show yourself," she Commanded, throwing magic around her room.

From downstairs came laughter. "Young lady, you're amusing. I haven't the faintest interest in watching you change clothes."

"Well, good!" she said hotly and slammed her door. She felt insulted.

She put on fresh jeans and grabbed a yellow t-shirt that said, "Do I look like I'm listening?" She held it, thought a minute, and tossed it back into the closet. Instead, she chose a pastel print pullover that felt like spring. It also seemed more adult.

She came downstairs to do her homework and found Damon seated at a table near the storeroom with a couple of her notebooks open in front of him. It seemed like such a contradiction, the remarkably handsome prince with his sword at his hip, studying her handwritten notes. Without asking permission.

94

"Did I say you could read my notebooks?"

"You didn't specifically forbid me to read your notebooks. Would you prefer me to hang around in your room?"

Annoying man. Prince. Creature. Whatever he is. "No."

She stepped into the storeroom and pulled her current notebook from the shelf, along with the geology textbook. Even if Uncle Roddyn was not going to review her notebook, she wanted to keep studying. It was her way of working to become an adult, and she had been at it for so long that her brain demanded the exercise

The next chapter in her text dealt with plate tectonics. She sat opposite Damon and opened her notebook to a fresh page. She used the spiral bound type of notebook so that she could pull out pages that she messed up on, because she used ball-point pens and couldn't erase her mistakes. She could have used pencil, but using a pen made her more careful when she wrote.

She had just begun to read about the different densities of rocks that made up the earth's crust when Damon spoke up. "Fascinating."

"What?"

"Your summary here about Earth's moon." He flipped some pages in her notebook. "It looks like you were studying astronomy during this notebook, and you wrote about the moon I have seen in your sky. We have no moon on my world. The sky was too close."

She put down her pen. "How strange. I can't picture a world without a moon in the sky."

"And how odd to me to have a moon the size of a planet circling the world. And your people have even walked upon it, using science instead of magic. We had kites on my world, but nothing else flew except birds. Certainly not people."

"Earth doesn't have much magic, not like worlds in the pocket universe. So we concentrated on the sciences."

"And yet you, Maddy, are a magical creature. How old are you?"

Her face grow warm. "I'm fourteen going on fifteen. Almost fifteen."

"Really." He closed his notebook with a snap. "That's a useful fiction." Nanny Bee walked in, perhaps by accident, and sat at their table. "Ah," said Damon, "the automaton returns."

"Don't insult Nanny," said Madison. "Be nice."

Damon flinched. "And don't you start issuing Commands again."

"Good morning," said Nanny Bee, looking calm and unruffled.

"Good morning, Nanny," said Madison.

Damon rose and bowed with royal pretension. "Good morning, Miss Bee, it is an honor." Madison rolled her eyes, and Damon sat back down and rested his arms on the table. "Miss Bee, how old is Madison?"

Nanny's eyes narrowed and she frowned. Madison stared at her. She almost never saw that expression on Nanny's face.

"Well?" said Damon.

"Don't, Damon," Nanny said. "Go amuse yourself somewhere else."

"But Madison wants to know. I want to know."

Madison glanced back and forth between their faces. Nanny definitely looked angry, and Damon had a thin smile on his face. His coal black eyes stared at Nanny without blinking.

"Nanny?" asked Madison. "Nanny, how old am I?" Her heart started pounding for some reason.

Nanny turned her face to Madison, her features now calm and unreadable. "Maddy dear, you are fourteen."

"But I had a birthday a couple of days ago; the vernal equinox is my birthday. Can't I be fifteen?"

"Not yet, dear."

"Tell me, Madison," said Damon, sitting back and flipping through the notebook he was holding, "How long does it take you to fill up a notebook?"

Nanny turned back to Damon. "Please. Do not do this."

96

"Um," said Madison, "I think about, oh, two months."

He tossed the notebook on the table. "Have you ever counted your notebooks?"

Madison's heart beat faster. "No. Once I'm done with a subject, I go on. Why would I ever want to go back?"

"Just to count?"

Madison stood up. "I need to get the kitchen ready for lunch."

"What's wrong?" asked Damon in a stronger voice. "Why won't you go back and count?"

"Damon, please," said Nanny. "Let it go."

Why not? What's wrong with my counting the notebooks? They're just sitting there. Why should I feel panic? Why can't I breathe?

"Yes," Madison said. "I suppose I could just go back and count them. I don't see why not." She clenched her fists, and the plastic pen in her hand snapped. She dropped it on the table and wiped ink from her hand with a napkin.

"Go work in the kitchen," said Nanny Bee. "I'll clean up here."

"No!" Madison grabbed her geology text. "I want to know. I'm going to count my notebooks." She turned towards the storage room, and Damon and Nanny Bee followed.

Madison pulled the door open and flicked on the light. She dropped her geology text on the book of Emily Dickinson poems, and passed her hand along the backs of the notebooks next to the texts. She was only into her second notebook for this year. Six notebooks made up the previous year. She pulled out the first of the six and glanced at the date to be sure. January. She pushed it back into place.

Five more notebooks completed the previous year, January to December.

Five more for the previous year.

Another six, then five, then another six.

Beyond them, four more sets of notebooks. Ten years total.

Her mouth was dry, and she couldn't swallow. She raised her hand to count the next set of notebooks, and saw that her hand was trembling.

"Come back out," said Nanny Bee. "I'll fix you some chocolate."

She shook her head. She counted out another set, and another. Twelve years.

But...

But...

She shook her head, trying to reason.

But if I am fourteen now, then twelve years ago I would have been...

Two. Two years old.

She yanked out the first notebook of the set from twelve years ago and almost ripped the cover getting it open.

"January," she whispered, looking at the date. "Famous Plays of Shakespeare." She closed it and pushed it back into place. She pulled out the next notebook and opened it. "March. Algebra. Factoring equations."

This was twelve years ago. I couldn't have been only two years old, not and do algebra. I couldn't...

She counted back another set of notebooks, and another, and another. She wiped her eyes with the palm of her hand, and counted five more years beyond that.

She put her hand on the notebook that marked the set from twenty years ago and looked at Nanny with anguish in her eyes. "Oh, Nanny...I'm over twenty years old! Twenty! And look at me!" She put her hands over her heart. "I'm still only fourteen!"

Nanny's expression didn't change. "I know, dear."

If Damon had meant to cause her grief, there was no satisfaction in his face, only a somber expression. "Finish what you started," he said quietly.

Madison whirled back to the notebooks and counted more sets, almost numb with shock, until she reached the end of the shelf. "Dear god above," she whispered, "I'm old. I'm forty years old! I've been studying for forty years!"

Damon started to speak, but Nanny interrupted. "No more, Damon. No more. Come away, Madison."

Damon shook his head. "Madison...the storeroom turns the corner. The bookshelf continues."

"No," whispered Madison. "It can't." She felt the openness beside her, the continuation of the storage room, like some dark monster that would never harm you if you never ever looked at it.

But she had to know. She had to know.

She turned, forcing herself, fighting with herself, and looked around the corner at the shelf which stretched into the back part of the storage room.

Notebooks.

Dozens and dozens of notebooks, dusty and untouched. She stumbled as she walked along them, running her hands over them as though she was blind. The binding changed from spiral bound to cloth bound and she pulled one out and opened it. The binding cracked as it opened and the pages were yellowed, but her writing was clear. "Basic English Grammar." There was a date at the top of the next page.

October 12, 1907.

She screamed and dropped the notebook as though it were a snake. Nanny put her arm around Madison and helped her out of the storeroom. She sat Madison down by the kitchen and got her a glass of water.

Madison spilled some of it as she tried to drink, and then set the glass down with a thump that spilled some more. She looked at Nanny with anguish. "Nanny! What am I? Am I an Escaped? How long have I been fourteen?"

Nanny sat beside Madison and held her hands with her cold, perfect fingers. "Madison, you are a human child. You were born here, and you absorbed the magic of this place. The blessing is that your body renews itself and you age slowly. But your memory also renews itself, and you only remember a few years back."

Madison wiped her eyes again and shivered. "But will I ever grow up? Won't I ever get older?"

"You age slowly, dear, but you will grow up."

"How many years? Do I have to wait another hundred years? Until Corey and every boy I ever meet dies of old age? How long do I have to wait? I'm sick of being fourteen!" The sobs fought their way out of her chest, and Nanny put her arms around Madison, pulled her head down against her shoulder and cradled her like a baby.

Nanny used her scold voice at Damon. "You see what you have done?"

"She had to know. I think it's important that she knows, especially now."

"She didn't need to get hit with it like that. And why now?"

"You heard Pinhead. Something has changed, and it's not just me arriving here. I was there when Pinhead explained about the origin of the pocket universe. I don't think the pocket universe is ever completely stable, and it wouldn't be now even if I went back. And that man she calls Uncle Roddyn is damaged and he isn't going to be able to deal with it. She's the only one, and I think she deserves to know as much as possible."

"Why do you care? Why should I think you are doing this for her benefit and not for your amusement?"

A pause. Madison was still shaking with sobs, but they were quiet sobs, and she listened to them speak.

"I don't know what I am," said Damon, "but certainly evil is self-serving as much as good. My fate is tied up with hers, and so is yours and everyone else's in this tavern. Everyone else in this universe, actually."

"My fate doesn't matter."

"Yes, yes, I know, you only exist to serve, and so forth. What a neat little philosophy you...ah...no, I can't continue. One

100

of her Commands was that I speak nicely to you, and I don't care to fight against it."

Madison felt Nanny's hands stroke her hair. "How are you doing, Maddy, dear? You've had an awful shock."

Madison sniffed, her nose clogged from crying. "Nanny, when was I born?"

"Oh, my dear girl, you don't want to know."

"Yes, I do."

Nanny rocked her a few times before saying, "The day you were born, your father scratched the year into the fresh concrete of the new stone fireplace."

She heard Damon rise and walk towards the fireplace. Could she remember the year? Pinhead had built the last fire in it last week, before the vernal equinox. There, on the side...

Damon walked back and sat down. "1824."

Madison drew in a shuddering breath and sat up. "No wonder. No wonder it feels like I've been fourteen forever. I was probably thirteen forever, too." She sniffed again, and Nanny pulled a paper napkin from the table's napkin holder and handed it to her. She blew her nose. "What about Uncle Roddyn?"

"Roddyn is an orphan. You were your parents' only child. It was your father who built the basement that enclosed the pocket universe, with my help."

"How long have you been here, Nanny?"

"One story at a time, dear. Your father was Elijah Parker, and he was born in England. Your mother was named Charity, and she was every bit as beautiful as you are, and they were both so very proud of their lovely daughter. Your father built your bedroom so that you could see the sunrise every morning."

Madison blew her nose again; her tears kept coming. "I'm going to forget their names again, aren't I? In a few years, I won't remember them again."

"You can remember them if you keep thinking about them, dear."

"I wish I had a picture of them in my room. Uncle Roddyn is sort of my parent, and you, you're like my mother so much that I never remember that I had a real mom and dad. Do we have any pictures of them? All I have is names but no faces. I can't remember anything about them."

Nanny shook her head. "I don't know of any pictures."

Madison folded the soggy napkin. "I'll dig through the old notebooks. Maybe I had one, once. Nanny, do you remember what they looked like?"

Nanny paused. "Your father was tall and thin, and his hair was always a horrible mess, like yours, and a rich brown color. He wore glasses and laughed a lot. Your mother was musical, and she had light hair and blue eyes. Before she died, she made me promise that you would do your studies and become a proper young lady."

"How did she die?"

"Now, dear, we all die. Your mother lived to a very old age. The best image I have of her in my memory was her singing while rocking your cradle. Maybe someday I'll figure out how to share that with you."

"What good are my studies if I don't remember anything?"

"You do remember, dear, and even if you forget Emily Dickinson, she will have influenced your mind. You are miles ahead of most fourteen year olds in your ability to think."

"Fat lot of good that does me."

"Think positive, young lady. Most things happen for a reason."

"In the meantime," said Damon, "since your study hour is pretty much ruined, you could go outside and walk with me for a bit. Frankly, red eyes and a red nose aren't very becoming to you."

"Why outside? And I don't care a fig what you think about my eyes and nose."

Damon put his hands on his hips. "Perhaps you could teach me that silly game with the disk which you toss back and forth."

Madison stared out the window at the sunshine, undecided. Mostly she wanted to climb into bed and pull the blankets up until she was buried forever.

"Oh, go ahead, dear," said Nanny. "It will do you good. I'll put your things away, and Mitch and Penny won't be here for an hour yet."

"Okay," said Madison, getting to her feet as though she was carrying a hundred pounds.

Damon opened the back door for her and smiled. "Age before beauty."

"Oh!" Madison glared at him. "I swear, I will find a way to get you back into your universe if it's the last thing I do!" Then she walked out into the back yard to teach the evil prince how to play Frisbee.

Chapter Eleven

Damon had difficulty catching the disk when Madison threw it to his left. His ornate sword on his hip kept interfering with his legs.

"Why don't you stick that sword in the ground?" yelled Madison. "You could catch things better."

"It's part of me," said Damon, "like my cape."

"So what? You won't lose it. It's not like you're going to need it, anyway."

"You don't understand." He trotted up to her, and she noticed that he was not out of breath. A normal person would be sweating from the exertion, but then, Damon didn't have lungs or a heart. "I really do mean that it's part of me. Here. I'll show you." He pulled out the sword, stuck it into the earth, and walked away several paces. "Now keep your eye on it."

She bent over and looked at the weapon carefully. The grip looked like it was made of woven cords of silver and gold, with an enormous pearl on the end of the hilt. The cross-guard was fine steel, and the edges of the blade gleamed in the sun. Writing was etched into the blade in an unknown language. "What does it say on the side of your blade?"

"Dragons Bane. There are common stories about that name in my world. I never have run into a dragon, though."

"It's hard to see. Actually, it's becoming transparent! Your sword, I mean. I can see right through it!" She reached out to touch it, and then drew her hand back. "It's gone!"

"Curses," said Damon in a light-hearted voice. "I lose more swords that way."

She stood up and saw that he had the sword on his hip again. "It returns to you?"

"In a way. It's actually part of my substance. Remember, when that young virgin transformed me, my essence became my form, and that included my cape and my sword and the rest. So it doesn't do me any good to, ah, Madison, what is that creature?"

She looked to where he was pointing, and saw something the size of a large dog waddling towards her on the grass. It had a long snout and large floppy ears, and if it weren't for the fur and thin legs, it would have looked like a tiny elephant.

"It's an Escaped." She rubbed her fingers together, wary. After Nashashuk, she didn't trust anything that passed into her world. She flicked a Common Tongue spell at it, but like the tree, it only whispered in her mind, and not even words but emotions. "It's afraid, and it's lost," she said.

The little creature stopped several feet from her and whined, raising its snout high and sniffing.

Damon drew his sword. "Do you need help?"

"No, no. Stay back." She wafted some peaceful magic at it, and said, "Come here, little guy. I'll help you get home."

The creature walked forward hesitantly, and sniffed at her ankles. Then it lifted its front feet and put them on her legs.

"It acts like it was somebody's pet," said Damon.

"It might have been." She reached her arms down, and felt acceptance from the creature. The fear from it lessened, and she picked it up. "Heavy, fat little thing. Smells like mustard, sort of. Come on, fella, let's take you home." It draped its snout over her shoulder and lay still in her arms. "Yes, it's used to being handled."

This should be a lot easier than getting Nashashuk back into the brane.

She stepped into the back door of the tavern and carried the creature to the wine cellar, but she was surprised to find that the door was already open. Uncle Roddyn stood at the shining brane, holding the Rat Witch's staff. "Oh!" she said. "You're up!"

He turned swiftly, his face startled. He lowered the staff and said, "Madison. You surprised me."

"I found an Escaped. Can you help me put him back?"

Roddyn shrugged. "Sure, if you want. I was trying to figure out how this staff works. It affects the brane. Watch." He swung the jeweled end until it touched the bright golden surface of the pocket universe. Instead of the staff being sucked in, the brane bulged outwards. "It's affecting the boundary somehow, and I think I need to get Pinhead to dress up again and explain it to me."

"Can we put this fellow back, though? He's getting nervous."

"Pick a world." Roddyn disengaged the staff and held it to one side so that Madison could approach the brane.

She glimpsed the worlds beyond, as they slowly shifted. It always fascinated her, the different landscapes. She was seeing them from above, looking down through their sky, and she often wondered if they could look up and see her looking down. For a time there were ocean waves, and then a wall like a soap bubble passed, and they were looking down on rivers and forests. Another world appeared, this one with tiny villages and an ocean shore.

The creature started wriggling, and she felt excitement in her mind.

"I don't know if he can smell it or sense it or what, but this world looks like it might be his." She lifted the animal from her shoulder.

"Wait a moment," said Roddyn. He lowered the gemstone end of the staff into the brane, and pushed. The terrain shifted, and beneath them appeared a hill, close enough that she could see flowers. "Now."

She put the creature on the floor, and it leaped into the brane. She saw it fall onto a bush, scramble to its feet, and trot off towards the village. Then the brane shifted to a desert scene with sand dunes.

106

Roddyn pulled the staff away. "The Escaped usually come to our universe from a mountain or hill close to their sky, and if their world has shifted, it can be quite a drop when they go back. And it's happening much more often than before." He brushed his mustache in thought. "Yes, indeed, I do have to get Pinhead to explain this staff to me."

"Are you feeling better?"

"A little, I suppose. Are Mitch and Penny coming today?"

"Any time now. It'll be a slow day; it's Monday. You should go rest."

"You're right, I should." He tucked the staff under his arm and closed the cellar door. He pushed the plaque that said WINE CELLAR back into place, and left for his bedroom without another comment.

"He used to be younger than me," said Madison thoughtfully. "I wonder if he remembers that? He never told me about it. Somehow we only talk about little things." Getting no response, she looked around. "Damon?"

He had vanished again.

Madison sighed, and went to the kitchen. Nanny Bee had set it up for making lunch, and Madison was just finishing the pot of soup – Mexican chili – as Penny and Mitch rode up.

They helloed at her as they entered the back door, and then Mitch walked through the tavern and unlocked the front door. Penny had on black slacks and a white blouse, and she tied an apron around her waist. The bar aprons were low and simple, right at the beltline, not like the cobbler's aprons in the kitchen that protected from spatters. Mitch had a couple of arm garters on his white shirt, and barely had time to tie his apron on before the first customer entered. It was ten o'clock.

From that point on they were modestly busy, enough to keep moving, which Madison appreciated. She was still staggered by learning – or re-learning – that she had been at The Padded Cell since the 1800's. She wondered why the customers didn't notice that she didn't age, but she guessed it was because they were wrapped up in their own lives, and maybe because most people don't think of themselves as aging and so don't expect it in others. She remembered customers talking about going to a high school reunion and being shocked to find their class was now a bunch of old people. "When did that happen?" they would say.

Mrs. Regan has got to be aware that she's been bringing textbooks to me for years and I haven't changed, and yet she's never mentioned it. I bet people's memories are affected by this place also. Pinhead can put on costumes and become someone different as part of his magic, so maybe that's part of my magic, that no one notices me not aging.

And I'm still fourteen going on fifteen. Or fourteen going on fourteen. Again.

"Maddy," said Penny, stepping into the kitchen, "Mitch can't figure out how to replace the paper tape on that old cash register. I'll watch the kitchen if you'll go help him."

"You got it. Stir the chili so the bottom won't scorch, okay? I'll be right back." She hurried across the dining floor and ducked behind the bar. She popped open the side of the cash register and showed Mitch how to feed the new roll of register tape up behind the ink ribbon, and then snapped shut the side again.

"Howdy, Sheriff," said the lone customer at the bar.

Madison looked up, startled. Sheriff Gazzio stood at the door, his eyes hidden behind his reflective dark glasses.

She quickly stepped out from behind the bar and returned to the kitchen.

Mustn't run, I'll call attention to myself, but I should move fast before he notices me. Man, oh, man, what rotten timing.

"I fixed the tape," she whispered to Penny. "That new sheriff just walked in and I think he saw me behind the bar."

"He's a hard case," said Penny, shaking her head, which made her brilliant red hair shake even more. "Good old sheriff Carson would just look the other way. You're not doing anything bad."

Madison turned the heat off under the chili, took off her apron, and sat at Emtianal's booth while the sheriff bought a soft drink and walked out the door to his police cruiser. Exhaling, she put her apron back on and returned to working in the kitchen. She got busy making sandwiches and soon forgot about the sheriff's visit.

By two o'clock the customers had almost finished off the chili, and she put some in a bowl to take to Uncle Roddyn. Nanny Bee took Madison's apron and some soiled linens out to the work shed to do laundry, and Madison went up to her room to get her latest novel.

As she came down the stairs, she was startled to see Sheriff Gazzio and a woman in a state police uniform standing by the bar.

"There's Madison, Sheriff," said Mitch. "What's the problem?"

Gazzio didn't answer. He tucked his sunglasses neatly into his shirt pocket, and said to Madison, "Your full name is Madison Parker?"

"Yes," she said hesitantly. She glanced back and forth between Gazzio and the woman. Her name badge said KOERNER, and her shoulder patch identified her as a member of the state police. "Can I help you?"

Gazzio cleared his throat. "I've got a protective custody order from Judge Perlesky of the First Circuit Court. For your own safety, we need to put you into a foster home for a day or so."

"Protective custody? I don't understand." She stepped down onto the wooden floor and gripped the stair railing with her hand.

Gazzio pulled a folded piece of paper from his other shirt pocket, and held it up in front of him. "Being behind the bar during working hours as a minor, working at the bar as a minor, and working in the kitchen as a minor."

"Hey," said Mitch, who had come up behind the officers. "It's a family business. Kids can drive tractors on a farm when they're minors. It's the same thing."

"It's not the same thing," said Officer Koerner, speaking up for the first time. She had tightly clipped hair and a severe narrow face, and her hips were a bit ungainly for her uniform. "The state liquor laws are very explicit about it."

"Besides that," said Gazzio, pulling another piece of paper from his shirt pocket, "we also have a truancy warrant."

"I told you before," said Madison, gripping the railing even tighter, "I'm being homeschooled."

Gazzio tucked the two warrants back into his pocket. "There's no notarized affidavit registered with the Sharonville school district, Miss, and no record of a proper home school evaluation. Both of these warrants have to be cleared up, and Judge Perlesky has determined that this is an unsuitable and unsafe environment for a minor."

Officer Koerner put a smile on her thin face. "Really, Madison, it will be like a vacation. We have a wonderful home for you to stay at, it's actually a ranch and they love kids, and they have horses to ride."

Sheriff Gazzio extended his hand towards the front door. "Come with us, Miss. Someone else can bring a suitcase for you with your things in it."

Madison slid her arm through the railing and anchored herself. "I can't go. Really. I'll promise to stay in my room, I'll sleep outside, but you can't take me away."

Gazzio shook his head. "It's not like you have a choice. Do you know what a warrant is, young lady? You are in protective custody, and you do have to come with us. The sooner your guardian clears this up, the sooner you'll be home."

"What needs clearing up?" Roddyn stepped into the room and leaned on the bar. "What's the trouble?"

Sheriff Gazzio handed him the two warrants. "We're putting Miss Parker into a foster home in protective custody for a few days, Mr. Roddyn, until these matters are cleared up. Judge Perlesky will hurry the hearing so she won't be gone long."

Roddyn looked at the warrants as though they were in a foreign language. "But you can't take her away. She's always worked here, you know, and it's never been a problem before. And she is being home schooled. I just didn't know about the notarized thing."

"Judge Perlesky will be happy to settle the case quickly, Mr. Roddyn. In the meantime, we will be leaving now with Miss Parker."

"Come on, now," said Mitch, "you can't do that. You..."

Gazzio put his hand on one of the thick black pouches at his hip. "Is there going to be a problem here, sir?"

Mitch put up his hands and backed away. "No, sir, sheriff, no problem, I was just saying."

"Come along, Madison," said Koerner, her smile still in place.

"I can't." Panic made her breathing shallow. "I really, really can't. You don't understand."

The smile disappeared. "Miss Parker, we don't want to put you in handcuffs for resisting arrest. You're not a criminal. Just come quietly with us to the car. You don't want to make a scene, do you?"

Madison slowly released her arm and pulled it away from the railing. "I've never been away from this place. I don't know what will happen. I'm frightened."

The smile returned. "It's just a wonderful vacation, Madison. There's no reason to be alarmed. You'll be back soon." She put her arm through Madison's arm, and led her towards the door. The contact was light, but Madison could tell that Officer Koerner was prepared to restrain her if she tried to run.

Madison looked back at Roddyn in desperation. "Uncle Roddyn? Can't you make them leave me here?"

Roddyn shrugged and lifted his hands in helplessness.

Uncle Roddyn gave up! I've never known him to give up! What's wrong with him?

The female officer led her out of the tavern's front door and down the long walk to the parking lot, half-supporting her because Madison could barely walk. Once at the car, the woman opened the back door and guided Madison inside. The back seat was black durable leather and smelled of cigarette smoke and sweat. A thick glass panel provided a barrier between the front and the back seat, and when she tried the door handles on both back doors, neither one would open. It was a cell.

I can't run away. There's nowhere I can run to. There's nowhere I can hide.

I could jump into a brane into another world, maybe, if I could get out and run.

But like Nashashuk, she might find herself in a lonely place, or she might fall and die if the brane wasn't over a mountain. And she couldn't get out now anyway, even if she put the two officers to sleep; the doors wouldn't open.

She tried with all her might to get calm, to think, to figure out some way to persuade the officers to let her stay behind, but Sheriff Gazzio sat down behind the wheel, and Officer Koerner sat down in the front passenger seat, and the motor started.

"Just relax, Madison," said Koerner. "Put on your seat belt and enjoy the ride. You'll be in your own bedroom at the ranch before you know it."

Madison realized that she still had her novel in her hand, and she dropped it on the seat. She didn't put on her seat belt. She turned around and looked back at the tavern as they reached the highway, and Mitch and Penny were standing outside the door, holding each other's hands. Uncle Roddyn wasn't visible.

The police cruiser turned left, and now she was further away from the tavern than she had ever been in her life. She rubbed her fingertips together, and nothing happened.

No magic.

The female officer looked back at her, her eyes evaluating Madison's demeanor. Satisfied that their prisoner was not harming herself, she turned forward and began chatting with Sheriff Gazzio, the thick glass barrier blocking their conversation.

Out the right window Madison could see Mount Majestic. Out the left window she saw a meadow with cattle in it. No matter how hard she looked behind her, though, she couldn't see the tavern any more.

She felt weak and thin. Her magic was gone, and a tiredness filled her.

The woman in front turned around, and spoke through a microphone on a coiled black wire. "How are you doing, Madison? We'll be there in half an hour."

Madison nodded, too weak to speak.

The woman turned back to the front, and accidentally left her microphone on. "Poor kid looks tired and scared, and she's thin as a rail. I didn't notice that in the tavern; I guess the light was bad. Anorexic, maybe, or maybe they really were mistrea…"

Sheriff Gazzio pointed to the microphone, and the woman hung it up.

Anorexic? Thin?

She never gained any weight, but she wouldn't have described herself as thin.

She lifted her arm, and studied it.

I am thin. I'm all skin and bones.

She ran her hand over her cheeks, feeling how bony they were, and then noticed Sheriff Gazzio looking at her through the rear-view mirror.

She looked out the right window, and then scooted over as though interested. She didn't like him staring at her.

Muscle and blood, skin and bones, a mind that's weak and a back that's strong….

The Jug and Fiddle Band singing Sixteen Tons ran through her head, and she held on to the music as she looked out at the fields passing by. Farmhouses, country stores, gas stations. Things she had never seen before, only read about in books.

She glanced at her hand again, and it scared her, so she looked quickly out the window and sang some more in her head.

Saint Peter, don't you call me, 'cause I can't go, I owe my soul to the company store....

She rested her forehead against the glass, and felt her body relax. She stopped blinking, but the land around her continued to unfold. She saw a stream, and a house with a white picket fence where a dog chased a boy, and a small restaurant with a big sign that said EATS.

Some trees flowed past, and a plowed field with something green starting to sprout. Then she saw a horse, a horse with a white blaze on its forehead, and something about the horse was so peaceful that she had to drift over to it.

She came to a stop in front of the horse, and it nickered and stepped back, white showing around its eyes.

Dear horse, don't be shy. I've never touched a horse before.

She reached out again, but it danced away and trotted across the field.

Her hand caught her attention.

It was no longer bones, it was back to its full shape, but it had no color, just a translucent white. She looked down at herself and saw that her feet were bare. She seemed to be wearing a thin white shift that came down to her elbows and ankles.

How odd. What happened to my sneakers?

A car went by on the highway, and she tried to remember why that was significant. Hadn't she been riding in a car? But why would she be doing that? She never left home, ever, not since she was born.

She ought to go back home. She should.

She thought about moving across the field, and so she did. It took no effort; all she had to do was to picture herself moving, and she moved. She went up and over a fence, and smiled. It was like flying. The next fence she didn't bother going over; she just went through it, and there was no resistance.

114

Which way was home?

The sun was getting low, so she ought to be getting home. Somebody might be looking for her.

She traveled, but she dawdled. A patch of blue flowers caught her eye, and she watched the bees bustling about them. She tried to catch one, but it buzzed out of her clenched fist.

The sun set, and the stars came out. She still had no idea which direction her home was but she could see fine; everything had a different sort of color to it.

She drifted through a barn, and saw a house with a light on upstairs. She was curious, so she slipped in through the closed front door, and looked at the furnishings. There was a bookshelf with books, and she wanted to pull one out and look at it, but again she couldn't grasp it.

What good is it if I can't touch things?

She tried rubbing her fingers together, but she had no magic. If there was a trick to touching things, she wasn't able to figure it out.

She heard a short scream, and turned around.

Halfway down the stairs stood a woman in a night robe, her hair in a cap. "Harry!" the woman cried in a strangled voice. "Harry, come quick!"

Madison stayed where she was, and waited for Harry to stumble around upstairs until he came down behind the woman. He mumbled some cuss words and stared at her just like the horse had. They both looked so funny that Madison laughed. It came out as a faint echo of a laugh, and the couple both backed up a step.

"Who are you?" the woman asked. "What do you want?"

"My hooome," said Madison faintly.

Ah, snap, I sound just like that tree.

"No," said the woman, "this is our home. We bought it."

"Go away," said Harry.

Madison looked down at herself again, pale and translucent, just like Étienne and Watseka had appeared.

115

I'm a ghost.

No, I'm not! I am absolutely not a ghost!

Out of spite, she flung her arms up and cried out, "Boooo!" As the couple scrambled back up the stairs in fright, she turned and drifted out through the wall.

Home.

How could she find her home?

She rose higher into the air, and looked out over the landscape. Nothing looked familiar, but in the distance, on a hill, she could see a campfire. There were people around the fire, and maybe they would know where her home was.

She dropped down to the earth, overshot, and didn't stop until she was several feet underground.

Interesting.

She could sense the different rock strata, and the deep roots of trees, and burrows of animals. She traveled along underground, enjoying the small undiscovered byways of water, the tiny caverns, the forgotten and filled-in wells.

She could tell that she was now under the fire, and she rose up slowly. No reason to burst up out of the ground. Of course, it probably wouldn't comfort the circle of people to have her rise up out of the fire, no matter how slowly, but she did it anyway.

Boy scouts. She could tell by their uniforms.

Some of them scattered, their marshmallows forgotten, graham crackers and pieces of chocolate left by the fire. Others, more brave, huddled and watched the apparition hovering in the flames.

One older scout grabbed the sleeve of a man, presumably the Scoutmaster, and shouted, "How did you do that? That's way cool!"

"Didn't do it," said the Scoutmaster, backing up slowly. "Wasn't me."

"Home," said Madison as loud as she could. "Where is home?"

"She's talking!" said the scout, hanging on to the reluctant Scoutmaster. "Listen! She's saying something!"

"Where is hooome?" she repeated. No matter how much she tried, her voice barely rose above a whisper.

"Home? Which home?" asked the scout. He had glasses and acne, but he looked almost as old as Corey.

Of course, they all have a home. Everybody has a home. What would they know about that's near my home? I remember that there was a mountain nearby. What was the name of that mountain?

There was a flash, and a short scout with a dumpy shirt ran away yelling, "I got a picture! I got a picture!"

"Where is the mountainnn?" she asked. "I need to go to the mountainnn."

"Mount Majestic?" said the scout. "You want to go there?"

"Yes! Where is Mount Majessstic?"

The older man looked around, trying to orient himself, and pointed in a direction. The scout said, "No, it's over that way more." They both pointed, and when Madison concentrated, she could make out the shape of the mountain in the distance.

She drifted out of the fire and came close to the Scout, who stood his ground though he trembled. "Thank you," she said. She wanted to say something meaningful.

What do Scouts do?

Something that she had read once finally came to her. "Beee an Eagle Scout," she said, waving her hands at all the cowering young men. "Obey the Scout Lawww...Or else!"

She turned in the direction of Mount Majestic and drifted off into the night, leaving behind a troop of boy scouts fervently committed to achieving the rank of Eagle.

Chapter Twelve

Mount Majestic rose before her, a silhouette against the starry night. She was weary, and she had lost all reference points. She just wanted to get somewhere and quit thinking. She drifted into the foot hills, passing through layers of ancient lava flow and contorted rock. She descended as she moved towards the center of the mountain, no longer caring where she went, only wanting to rest.

Her memories faded and her identity faded. Her name vanished. She was just a consciousness moving like a slow spark into the heart of the ancient mountain.

There was great heat below her, and it called to her. She wafted deeper under the mountain and found a column of lava, glowing a dull red. The mountain was not dead, only sleeping. The lava comforted her, and she settled into the column of warmth like it was her own bed. It was peaceful and warm, and she was content.

She relaxed, and slept within the mountain's deep hot blood.

Move.

"Uh." She grunted. Why was Nanny always waking her up, just when she was most comfortable?

I said, move.

"Uh." The light around her was a dull red; it wasn't sunshine. Nanny was waking her up too early.

Something pressed against her, something sour and dark.

Get moving, Madison, before you vanish!

The voice, the darkness, was pushing her out of the comfortable warmth.

How annoying. It couldn't be Nanny.

That's right, little girl. That's the direction. Faster.

She didn't want to go faster, but she had no will of her own any more, and if the darkness said to go faster, she would go faster. She passed through rippled rock and buried lava tubes, plant roots and shattered stone. She emerged from a rock wall, and the morning sunshine hit her.

"Uh." The sunlight was a palpable pressure, and she felt as though she was swimming upstream. A cloud of darkness pressed against her back, helping her move against the light.

There, across the highway, is the tavern. Can you see it?

Tavern?

They passed over treetops, and ahead stretched a highway. She wanted to go back to the warmth in the mountain, but the darkness wouldn't let her.

Don't quit now, Madison. You have to move fast when we get near the tavern, because I'll get solid again.

What a silly thing to say, get solid again. Nothing made sense.

They passed over the highway to a side road with trees on both sides. At the end of the side road stood a large two-story building that looked familiar.

Go to your room. Do you hear me? Go to your room and lie down on your bed.

Her room. Did she have a room?

Go upstairs to your room, Madison! Go!

119

With one last push, the darkness behind her fell away. She drifted into the wall of the building. Go upstairs, the darkness had told her, go upstairs, and so she rose up until she came to a bedroom with the sun shining into it.

She stood in the middle of the bed with her feet near the wooden floor. Lie down, the darkness had said. She concentrated, and rotated until she was horizontal over the bed. She dropped a bit until she was level with the quilt, and decided that was good enough.

There. Now maybe everyone will just leave me alone.

She would have preferred the lava bed in the mountain's heart, but this bed seemed acceptable.

She closed her eyes.

Drip.

Drip.

"Don't move, dear, if you can hear me. You're very delicate right now."

Drip.

Delicate? What keeps dripping?

"I'm putting drops of milk into your mouth, Madison. Your body is trying to recreate itself, but it's got nothing to work with. Don't chew, don't swallow."

I'm home?

She felt nothing. Well, not quite nothing. There was a tapping at the back of her throat that matched the dripping sound she heard.

"Don't move, dear. Don't try to answer me. Just be still, don't try to open your eyes, and be very, very patient."

Be still, be patient. Be good, be trustworthy, be loyal, be courteous, be kind, and help other people at all times.

I'm home.

How did I get home? And why wasn't I at home already?

Drip. Drip. Drip.

"Don't move, dear, if you can hear me. You're very delicate right now."

Message repeats. That's Nanny.

"Astonishing, and I have seen many strange sights in my life." Damon's voice.

Madison wasn't supposed to open her eyes. Did she even have eyes? She didn't even feel muscles that she could twitch to open her eyes. No eyelids. No eyes. Blinder than a fruit bat.

"It's her magic," said Nanny Bee. "But I did not know that she could come back from this, that she could come back from nothing."

"That's the most horrible looking thing I…"

"Damon, I have never hurt a creature in my existence but if you finish that sentence it will be completely within my parameters to injure you in every possible way."

Drip. Drip. Drip.

Nanny Bee spoke again. "Where did you find her?"

"Floating in the middle of that mountain. There wasn't much of her left."

"How could you locate her?"

"I could sense her once I left the boundaries, though I'm not sure why. Perhaps it's because she's the only interesting person around here and I've been watching her for several days, or perhaps because she's Commanded me enough that I feel a link to her. She was reluctant to move. I think she was becoming part of the mountain."

"Thank you, Damon, for getting her."

Drip, drip, drip.

"So she's recreating all her inner parts? Bones, muscles, everything? She's a living lesson in anatomy. Okay, okay, I'll stop talking about it."

"Don't move, dear, if you can hear me. You're very delicate right now."

Madison couldn't help it. She tried to twitch her leg, but nothing responded, nor would her fingers move.

When I was drifting around, I could move just fine. Now I'm, what, recreating my inner parts? It's like I'm trapped again.

"Damon, I'm going to need more milk. Would you please get another gallon from the kitchen?"

"What about meat? Or bread?"

"She needs the liquid and the calcium to make her bones." Her voice dropped to a whisper, but Madison could still hear her say, "Eventually, when she recreates her teeth, we can give her solid foods."

Madison tried hard not to make a mental picture of herself, a partial skeleton with traces of blood vessels and muscle holding it together, no lips, no teeth. She must be a horrible sight.

Muscle and blood, skin and bone...

The lyrics from Sixteen Tons began playing in her head again. Her mind was pulling itself together. She understood that she was in her room, and she remembered now that she had been taken away, away beyond the boundaries of the tavern, beyond the influence of the pocket universe. She had been born here in the tavern; her essence was woven with the ever-present magic from the little universe.

Had she died? She had been taken away by the police, and while riding in the car, had become unraveled. She had drifted.

Someone...Damon...had found her, and helped her get home.

Footsteps returning. Damon with more milk.

No, two sets of footsteps. Who was with him?

A gasp, and she recognized who made that gasp. It was Penny. "What is this? What's going on?"

122

"Please," said Nanny. "Miss Rusting, don't come in here. Please. Madison is trying to come back to us, and you shouldn't be here."

"But the sheriff took her away."

"That's right, but the sheriff returned last night right after you and Mr. McKenzie closed up and left. He was very upset, and asked if Madison had come back. The sheriff had her clothes in his hand, and said that when they got to Sharonville there was nothing in the back seat but dust and clothes and a book. We must not let him find out that Madison is here."

"That, that thing on the bed, that's Madison?"

Yep, that's me.

The music in her head continued.

If you see me coming, better step aside. A lot of men didn't, and a lot of men died...

"It's trying to be Madison," said Nanny. "Please, Miss Rusting. Forget about what's up here. Go downstairs and open the tavern and if people ask, tell them that Madison was taken away by the sheriff and we haven't seen her since."

"But what if the sheriff comes back again? He will, you know, and that lady cop. Those two will try to find her, they'll hunt for her."

Silence.

That's true. They won't stop looking for me.

Damon spoke up. "We should move her to another room. They'll come upstairs and look in here, and if she successfully rebuilds her body, they'll try to take her away again."

"I don't know if we dare move her yet," said Nanny.

"I'll go back downstairs," said Penny, "but please, let me know how she's doing?" Footsteps, and Madison assumed that Penny was gone.

"Here's what we can do," said Nanny. "We will lift up the quilt, you and me at each end, and we will move her to Pinhead's room. I think if we are careful, we won't hurt the process. Pinhead can sleep in here."

123

"Now you're starting to think devious thoughts, Nanny. There's hope for you yet."

She heard rustling as the corners of the quilt were gathered, and then swaying as she was moved.

"Her spirit and her body are barely connected," said Nanny. "Move slowly."

After more rustling, she was still again. She must be on Pinhead's bed.

"Thank you for the milk," said Nanny, and the dripping began again. "If you can hear me, dear, don't move. You are very delicate right now."

There came a point where she could breathe, and about the same time she felt a tremulous heartbeat begin. Nanny was putting broth into her mouth now, something with different nutrients, something that would allow her to rebuild her blood and muscles.

"How do you know to do this?" asked Damon.

"I have been with Madison since she was a baby. She has had some bad injuries over the decades. I know what helps her heal."

"Fascinating. Look, there's skin starting to form over her..."

"Damon, do not speak of it. I am sure that she can hear us."

"Really? Without ears?"

"Watch her hand. Madison, dear, if you can hear me, please move your hand just the tiniest bit."

Madison tried to make a little twitch, failed, and tried harder.

"There," said Nanny. "We saw that, Madison, that's enough. Now lie still some more. I know it is hard for you, but time must pass. This can't be hurried."

Heavy footsteps. More than one person was coming up the stairs. Madison heard Uncle Roddyn's voice. "Sure, look anywhere you want to, again. I told you she hasn't come back. I still don't know how you lost her in the first place."

"That's still being investigated." It was Sheriff Gazzio.

"Investigated?" Officer Koerner's voice, and she sounded angry and distraught. "Investigated? You've got police keeping watch for an anorexic fourteen year old girl who's running around naked, and you call that an investigation?"

"Janet, please, not here...."

"What you need to investigate is how a young girl can throw off her clothes and climb out of your back seat with the doors and windows locked and the cruiser doing sixty miles per hour. Explain that!"

"I can't!" he snapped. "Now save it for later. If we can find her, then she can explain it herself. This is her room." Through the wall, she could hear her closet door being opened and her shower curtain being pulled to one side. Footsteps in the hallway, and then Pinhead's door opened with a squeak and people walked into the room where she lay.

"Please don't disturb my patient," said Nanny Bee. "I'm from hospice. Mr. Roddyn, I told you that she mustn't be disturbed."

Roddyn stuttered. "I...I..."

Sheriff Gazzio spoke quietly. "I'm sorry, I didn't know that someone here was terminally...ah, that someone here was ill. Was this woman here last night?"

"Yes. I was sitting here with her. I heard you pass, but I was grateful that you didn't wake her."

"I could have sworn I looked..." A moment's pause. "What's wrong with her?"

"Extreme old age. She was the previous owner's wife, and the deed said that she could stay here until she passes on. You can look wherever you need to, but for her sake, please don't touch any surfaces and please be brief."

"I won't disturb her. She looks...this will only take a moment." Madison heard the sheriff step quickly to look in the bathroom and closet. "Nothing," he said.

"I can't believe you didn't check this room last night," said Koerner.

"Let's go." They left the room and walked down the stairs, whispering angrily to each other.

"Hospice?" asked Roddyn.

"I will explain later," said Nanny. "Please go with the sheriff."

Roddyn left, and Nanny went back to feeding Madison broth.

"Well, well," said Damon. "You tell lies as though you were born to it."

"And you disappear very conveniently. I do not have a fast body, Damon, but I am swift at thinking."

Another spoonful of broth landed at the back of Madison's throat, and she actually swallowed.

Madison heard Nanny Bee's footsteps but tried to ignore them, to stay in the peaceful dream that supported her. She was floating on air and resting peacefully. Why did Nanny have to break into her sleep?

Nanny spread wide the bedroom curtains, letting in the early morning sunshine.

126

"Ack!" Madison settled a couple inches onto her bed. "Nanny!"

"Yes, dear?"

"Can't you just let me sleep in for once?"

"The early bird gets the worm, dear. It's going to be a beautiful sunny day."

Madison gasped, coming fully awake. She had eyelids! She had eyes! She raised her arms and looked at her hands. They were terribly thin but they had skin on them, and her bones were solid. She touched her cheeks, feeling how thin her face was.

She was so hungry, she could eat a horse. Well, not a horse. She had almost touched a horse. Maybe she was so hungry she could eat a cow. "I'm starving."

"Of course you are, dear. Let me prop you up, and I'll feed you some soup."

"I want a steak and fries. Hey, I lisped! What in the world?" She stuck her finger into her mouth, and felt her gums. No teeth. She moaned in frustration. "Okay, fine, soup. Lots of soup."

"It's ham and pea soup, and it's not very hot. Last night I asked Penny to make some soup before she left, and this was what she came up with. It's healthy, but I don't know how it will taste."

"Anything will taste good. Dishwater would taste good." She slurped the first spoonful that Nanny offered and dripped some. "Can I feed myself? And it could use more salt."

Nanny put a towel under Madison's chin. "I'll hold the bowl for you, dear. See if you can use the spoon."

Madison managed to get most of the soup into her mouth before taking the bowl with both hands and drinking it down. "More," she asked.

"In a bit. You have a new stomach, and it's probably very small."

Madison ran her hands from her ribs to her hip bones. Her abdomen caved in like it was hollow. "Scary. I wonder what my pant size is now? I bet I've got a 12 inch waist."

She heard slow footsteps coming up the stairs. She touched her fingers together, and was comforted by feeling the magic.

And Damon is in the room, I can feel him, and surprisingly, I don't mind. He may be evil inside, but he did come get me.

There was a knock at the door, and Uncle Roddyn put his head in. "May I come in?"

"Yes," said Madison, happy to be able to speak.

Roddyn stepped into the room, sat down in Pinhead's single sturdy chair, and rested the Rat Witch's staff across his lap. He shook his head. "If I didn't know it was you, I wouldn't have recognized you."

Madison was struck by the change in Roddyn's appearance. She couldn't put her finger on it – he had the same gray hair pulled back into a ponytail, the same long gray mustache under his veined nose, the same massive shoulders and small hands. Yet, somehow, he seemed different, darker, as though part of his vitality had been replaced by something less trustworthy.

"Have you seen yourself?" he asked.

She shook her head.

Nanny spoke up. "She's still re-growing her body. It doesn't matter what she looks like right now."

Madison looked about the room. There were no mirrors; Pinhead had no concerns for his appearance. The only mirror would be over the sink in the bathroom. "Nanny, could you get me the hand mirror from my room?"

"I don't see any benefit in that," said Nanny. "What you look like right now is not the real you."

"I want to see. Could you, please?"

Nanny nodded reluctantly and stepped out of the room.

"I thought you were gone for good," said Roddyn. "Things are getting out of hand."

"Damon came and helped me get back here. I think I fell asleep in the middle of the mountain. The sheriff must have had a fit when he got to Sharonville and I wasn't there anymore."

Roddyn nodded. "Sheriff Gazzio was very upset and totally baffled. I was as polite as I could be, I let him look everywhere, even woke up Pinhead checking in this room. The sheriff walked down into the wine cellar, even; I'm glad I had it set for that. Of course, I didn't know anything about what had happened to you either, except that you were gone, and he was carrying your clothes. I thought you had vanished, literally. I should have known you were more resilient than that."

"When he took me away, I just unraveled, sort of. I was a ghost for a while." She held up her arm and looked at it. "I still feel like a wraith or a zombie or something. What are you doing about serving lunch?"

"Oh, I put a sign up saying the bar was open, but the kitchen was closed until 4 pm. Mitch and Penny are doing a good job. I haven't done any work yet; I'm still too washed out."

Madison nodded.

It doesn't feel like Uncle Roddyn is in charge any more. I might be on my own.

Nanny came back with an oval hand mirror with a blue plastic handle. Madison took it and angled it so that she could see her face. She moaned. "Look at my mouth, like an old woman's. My cheeks, my eyes, and my hair! Look at my hair!" She reached up and took hold of the wispy hair hanging down onto her forehead, tugging it in disbelief that it was actually hers. It was almost pure white.

She tried to cry, but she didn't have tears yet, just waves of heartache. She drew back her hand to throw the mirror against the wall, but instead she only handed it back to Nanny, her face twisted in grief.

"Oh, Madison dear, it will grow in properly." Nanny crouched beside her bed and put her hand on Madison's shoulder. "Give your body time. You won't stay this way."

"I'll let you rest," said Roddyn, standing. He started to say something else, shook his head, and left with his shoulders slumped.

129

"Don't let anyone else see me," said Madison, gripping Nanny's hand. "Please? Not Penny or Mrs. Regan or Pinhead or anyone."

"I won't, dear. Should I go get you some more soup?"

"Yes, please." She wanted to blow her nose, but without tears, she didn't even have the sniffles. "Thank you. Then maybe I can grow some teeth back. I'm such a mess."

Nanny left the room, and Madison laid her head back on her pillow and closed her eyes. Pinhead's bed was lumpy, but she was so light it didn't matter. "Damon? I know you're here."

"Yes, I'm here."

"You're the only one allowed to see me. You saw me when I was just bones and blood vessels."

He snorted. "Thank you for your permission. You were a sight, yes, and right now you really do look like an old woman, except that your skin is like a newborn."

She opened her eyes and saw that he was visible and standing beside her bed, his black pageboy hair perfect as usual and a smirk on his excessively handsome face. "I can't figure out if I should kick you for being mean," she said, "or hug you for rescuing me."

"Kicking me would be your best choice. I'm not fond of sickly sentimentality. In fact, I think I'll wander off while you eat that soup. Not being able to eat or drink myself, I find it dull to watch others indulge."

"Thank you, anyway, for getting me."

"I'm a prince," he said with a sour expression. "It's what I do." He turned and left the room.

Nanny returned, helped Madison down another bowl of soup and as much milk as she could handle, and let her sleep again.

Madison woke around noon. She was tired of sleeping – though that seemed a contradiction – and she wanted to walk outside and enjoy the spring sunshine.

She felt inside her mouth with her finger. Little bumps showed that her teeth were developing.

I'm teething. Joy of joys. I'm glad I'm already potty trained.

It seemed dark outside for noon, and she slipped out of bed and looked out the window.

Snow was falling.

Chapter Thirteen

Snow.

Snow was still possible in March, yes, certainly it was, but after a sunny morning and yesterday being so warm, it didn't feel right to Madison. If she looked towards the orchard, she could see bare earth beneath the trees. The snow began partway through the orchard, and intensified close to the tavern.

She got out of bed and grabbed her Levis, but they were too loose to stay up. As she started to thread a belt into the belt loops, she noticed her bony arms and remembered her appearance. She stepped into Pinhead's bathroom and looked at herself in the mirror over the sink. Her hair was still white, her mouth toothless, and her face cadaverous.

I can't go downstairs looking like this.

The bottom of the stairs was visible from the tavern, and if there were any customers it would be hard for her to sneak out unnoticed. She thought of carrying a broom and waving her arm while crying, "Double, double, toil and trouble, fire burn and cauldron bubble!" That would be fun, but she really didn't want to draw attention to herself, not now.

Damon. He could help out.

"Damon, are you here?" she called. She couldn't sense him in the room, and where was Nanny when she needed her? She didn't want to yell; it would bring up Penny or Mitch.

She lay down on the bed in frustration.

Pinhead showed up, though. He stopped at the door of the room – his room – and put his finger in his mouth. "Who are you?"

"Me? Oh, I'm...uh..."

I look nothing like the Madison he knows, and I'm not up to explaining it to him.

"I'm looking for Nanny Bee," she said. "If you see her, could you send her here?"

"Hm. Okay. You're in my room."

"Nanny will help me get to the right room, okay?"

"You're on my bed."

"Nanny will get me to the right bed. Go get Nanny."

"Okay." He looked doubtful, but went back down the stairs.

She watched out the window as Pinhead walked through the snow towards Nanny's shed. Nanny was probably doing laundry again, and sure enough, Madison saw Pinhead returning with her. He had a coat on but Nanny still wore only her pinafore apron and work dress. In moments, Nanny appeared at her door.

"You needed something?" Nanny asked as she brushed snow from her hair and shoulders.

"It's snowing."

"That's obvious, dear."

"But I think it's only snowing next to the tavern."

Nanny looked out the window. "Yes, you're right. I should have noticed it at the shed."

"Is Uncle Roddyn using the Rat Witch's staff again? I remember that it shifts the seasons, like it did with the cherries. It will look strange to everyone to have it snowing just around the tavern only, like we're a holiday snow globe or something."

"I'll go down and see." Nanny went back down the stairs.

Madison started to pace, but found that she was too weak and hungry. She lay down on the bed and waited impatiently.

Light flashed outside, and suddenly sunshine and a clear sky was visible outside her window. She looked out and once

133

again it was spring and the blanket of snow had begun to melt. Nanny came back upstairs. "Yes, he was experimenting. Mitch and Penny are getting quite an education about The Padded Cell."

"I hope Uncle Roddyn will be careful. We don't want this place to get a reputation. People think it's just an old-fashioned tavern with weird people running it."

"I'll mention it to him, dear, but he doesn't listen to me much. He never has."

"I'm worried about him. He looks different. Pinhead said that Nashashuk's lightning had damaged his nervous system."

Nanny nodded. "I also am concerned."

"Tell me about him. You knew him when he was an orphan, right?"

Nanny's expression went blank. "Yes, but that's a story for another time."

"I'm lying here awake and I can't leave the room, so tell me. How did he get here, and who raised him?"

Nanny sat down on Pinhead's chair and looked at her as though evaluating what to say. "As to who raised him, it was a couple living here that you don't remember. After your mother and father passed away, there were other couples who took care of the tavern and who took care of you. Your parents trained others to take their place just like Penny and Mitch are learning about this tavern bit by bit. Little Roddyn arrived decades after your parents passed away."

"How did he arrive?"

"He appeared on the lawn behind the tavern on a winter's day, and almost froze to death before he was found."

"He was a baby?"

"He was little." Nanny focused on Madison, as though to gauge her reaction. "He wasn't human at that point."

"What?"

"He had scales, and a tail, and claws, but he was tiny and helpless, so the couple in charge of the tavern took pity on him and

134

took him in. As months passed he grew more human. By the time he was three, he looked like any human child."

"Uncle Roddyn had scales?" Madison pushed herself up to a sitting position. "You mean Uncle Roddyn is an Escaped?"

She nodded. "Yes, dear. At first he was like a child and you helped tend him, then he grew to be the same age as you and you would play rough and tumble games together, you would go fishing together in the stream. Then he got older and began tending bar and eventually took over the tavern. He's done a good job taking care of it and taking care of you."

"He should. He's the Caretaker." Madison rubbed the bony side of her forehead. "Pinhead said Uncle Roddyn's nervous system was different. I had no idea."

"You should treat him just like before, Madison, and don't mention anything I just said. I only tell you this because I am concerned about him."

And now Damon knows it, too.

She had sensed his presence in the room earlier when Nanny arrived, but hadn't mentioned it. "Nanny, I just thought of something. If I didn't have a brain, because I didn't have any body at all when I was a ghost, how come I still remember things now that I have a new brain?"

"I am just a machine, Madison, and there are some things to which no one knows the answer, but I have observed that there is something within humans that continues after their body dies. Think of Étienne and Watseka. Of course, in your case, I am not sure you really died; your body just became unraveled, as you so aptly put it. But knowledge passes between your body and your spirit in both directions, so your knowledge is never really lost."

"Then how come when I was just a spirit, I didn't remember more things? Can't my spirit remember everything?"

"Madison, you are a creature of both universes. You can't judge the capacity of your spirit from its behavior away from this place."

Madison lay back on the bed and stared at the ceiling. "That's a lot to think about. And I'm hungry again."

"Smile at me," said Nanny. "Big smile."

Madison made a wide open smile at Nanny, and Nanny nodded. "Just bumps, no teeth. I'll bring more soup."

"Soup. Phooey. At least add some more salt to it. Please?"

The evening passed without further incident. Madison, having left her previous novel behind in the sheriff's car, began reading *The Princess Bride*, a pleasant change from Agatha Christie and Raymond Chandler, and much more readable.

Damon made himself visible and reported on the doings downstairs: Mitch and Penny were fine; the cook with the hairy arms still complained a lot and insisted that she was not available at noon to make soup, and Emtianal would only play rummy with Damon, not poker, because the prince didn't have any money. "You see? If I had been evil, I could have arrived here with gold rings and pockets full of silver."

"Good people have money, too," said Madison, setting aside her book and picking up the argument.

"But they give it away."

"Perhaps, but in return, they receive blessings that are more valuable than money."

"Ah-hah!" cried Damon, pouncing on a point. "Thereby showing that their so-called goodness is merely a device to acquire things, even if they are immaterial, such as a better pew, the praise of men, or positions of trust and power. Oh, yes, I know what it is to donate money and receive power and influence in return."

136

"I'm not talking about that. I'm talking about, like, leaving a loaf of bread at someone's door and running away so they can never say thank you. Unselfish actions."

"You think so? And what do they gain from such behavior? A feeling of superiority." He tossed back his cape and raised his arm, emphasizing his point. "Not only do I think that what we term 'evil' leads to prosperity, but that what we term 'good' is equally self-serving."

She shook her head in frustration. "You are so wrong, Damon."

"You want to kick me. Go ahead. It would make you feel better."

"I don't want to kick you. Actually, yes, I do, I want to kick you in the head if it would pound some sense into you."

He leaned towards her. "Command me to be good, Madison. I'm torn between the two paths, I'm of two minds, I can't stand the evil inside of me and I can't stand the goodness on the outside. You can't command me to be evil, that's not in your nature, but you can command me to be good."

"I don't think I can do that. You said yourself…."

"Just do it!"

And if I succeed? If he's totally good, will he still be drawn to me, the perpetual fourteen year old? Or will he go where he can be more useful?

I pity him, torn in two like that. Maybe I can heal him. Think positive, Madison, think positive, even if it means he might leave me, he saved my life and he deserves to be healed.

She drew in a deep breath and rubbed her bony fingers together, drawing deeply on her powers. Then she threw her magic at Damon, Commanding as strong as she could, "Be Good!"

He fell back onto Pinhead's sturdy chair, and shuddered. "Well thrown." He rested his hand on his chest and stared vacantly for a moment. "Still no heartbeat. No breath of air. I remain as I was. I'm sorry."

"I'm sorry, too. How will you ever resolve yourself?"

137

He looked down at his boots. "There is only one way, as I've known all along. I will need to decide, to choose a path. Me, myself."

"But most people are a mix of good and evil. Why do you have to be one way or the other?"

"Because that's the only way I will become a complete person." He rose to his feet, his face angry. "I want a heart that beats, and blood that flows, and that will happen only when I choose one path or the other, but I can't choose, Madison, I can't choose until I can convince myself that one path is superior to the other. You defend the good because of your nature, and I defend the evil because it's more logical, but in the end, I myself will have to know for certain." He struck his chest with his fist. "I have to know, deep inside, that the choice I am making is the only logical and true choice to make, that it's in my best interest. And right now, I can't do that. I can't decide, I can't choose! And until I can decide, I can't eat a biscuit, I can't drink wine, and I can't even spit!" He whirled and stomped from the room.

Madison listened to him go noisily down the stairs.

What is the secret? How do I let him know that good is better than evil? He's been immersed in both, but both failed him, it seems.

How do I know that I should be good? Me, Madison, how do I know that? I've always assumed it was the right way, but why?

She lay back down on the bed and stared at the ceiling. She was so deep in thought that she didn't hear the light footsteps coming hesitantly up the stairs.

What she did hear was a tentative knock on the door frame. "Hello?"

Madison lifted her head. It was Penny.

"Madison?" she asked, her hands clasped tightly as though they might run away. "Is that you?"

Madison sighed. "Come in, Miss Rusting. I mean, Penny. I didn't want you to see me like this."

Penny sat tentatively on Pinhead's sturdy wooden chair and studied Madison with a pensive expression.

That chair has pretty much held everyone in the tavern today except Emtianal, and I wouldn't be surprised to see him coming up the steps. Except Emtianal never leaves his booth.

"You're starting to look a lot like Madison," said Penny timidly, "but you look like you've been in prison for fifty years or something."

Madison put her arm over her eyes, symbolically hiding herself. "I know."

"Oh, I didn't mean to make you feel bad. Your hair looks lovely, really. It's very blonde."

"I look like a hag, but I'll get over it. I just need food and rest. Thanks for making that soup; I've been living on it."

"I was happy to do it. Can I bring you anything, a sandwich or a hamburger?"

Madison removed her arm, and looked at Penny's worried face. "I can't chew yet. No teeth."

"Oh, I'm sorry. I'm saying all the wrong things."

"No, it's not your fault. Tomorrow I'll be better, I just don't know how much."

"I hope so. I miss the bouncy Madison with an attitude that kept the place going."

With an attitude. I did not have an attitude. Much.

"I'll be back," said Madison.

"Oh, and I just wanted to be sure that you knew what Mitch and I just did."

"Did? What did you do?"

"Well..." She looked worried again. "Mitch and I are selling our store near the state capitol, the bike store, and we signed the papers with Roddyn to buy half ownership of The Padded Cell."

Madison lay silent, stunned.

How dare Uncle Roddyn sell the place! Or sell half the place, anyway, without consulting with me?

Because I'm a minor, that's why. I may be older than dirt, but I'm still only fourteen. I don't even have a driver's license. Which I will never get unless they come here to test me.

She clenched her jaw, trying not to say anything rash. Was there any problem about Mitch and Penny becoming part owners? They understood what they were getting in for, mostly. Some. After all, they had seen the ghost, they understood about Emtianal, and Penny was seeing Madison trying to recreate her own body.

Besides, Uncle Roddyn wasn't trustworthy anymore. Someone had to keep the tavern running, and Madison couldn't work behind the bar.

"That....that's great, Penny."

"You had to think about it though. Are you sure it's okay?"

"It got more okay the more I thought about it. Uncle Roddyn just never said anything to me about it."

"I figured that. I hope we didn't take advantage of him. I don't know who suggested it, but it just seemed the right thing for me to do." Penny rubbed her fingers together and a faint glow appeared. "Besides, I found out how to make our motors start every time. I guess we belong here!"

The next morning, she had teeth.

Nanny had brought her a glass of milk just before she went to sleep, and it must have been what her body needed. She looked in Pinhead's grimy mirror and smiled broadly, checking out her pearly whites. They looked wonderful, they felt wonderful, and she wanted to chew apples and carrots and fibrous and crunchy things.

Her hair was longer, and the roots were darker. Maybe she wouldn't stay a blonde after all.

She had hated her hair when it was almost white. Now that it was starting to grow in dark, she was distressed at losing her new look.

Maybe I'm fifteen! I'm having mood swings!

She turned sideways, and although her stomach was returning to normal – she could probably wear her Levis now – she wasn't developing anywhere else.

Fourteen, if that.

She was thin, but no longer cadaverous and anorexic. She grabbed a bar of soap and touched it to the corner of her eye. It stung, and her eye began watering.

Yes! I can cry! Now I need something to cry about.

Maybe The Princess Bride *has a tragic ending, and I can sob for a while.*

She was tempted to look ahead in the book, but then it wouldn't be tragic even if it was, so she didn't.

Instead she pulled on her pants and a t-shirt that said, "I wondered why the rock was getting bigger. Then it hit me." She went downstairs to enjoy being alive and having a body, even if it was only fourteen.

Emtianal was sleeping, so she stepped out the back and saw Nanny bringing back the wagon. "Nanny! I should have taken the garbage out. You should have woken me up."

Nanny put the wagon in its usual place before answering. "You needed your sleep, dear. My, you do look better. Almost healthy."

"Almost healthy. That's as bad as saying I'm almost beautiful."

"You are almost beautiful."

Madison made frog eyes and stuck her tongue out at Nanny.

I've got my attitude back.

"Have you seen any handsome princes knocking about?"

"No. He doesn't speak to me."

"How rude. I suppose I should start doing my homework and making soups again?"

"Are you sure you are comfortable with customers seeing you the way you are, and answering their questions?"

"Um…no." She fluffed her white hair. "I'm not. Maybe tomorrow I can be public. I better go back to my room and have you bring me my stuff."

"I can do that, dear."

"But first, I want to walk up the stream to the waterfall. I'll nap better if I exercise a little, and I need to get out and get some air."

"Go ahead and walk to the falls. I'll take your study materials up to your room."

Madison walked to the orchard – she wasn't up to running yet – and passed through to the fishing stream beyond. It was small enough that she could jump across it in certain places, and it had some native brook trout, too small to eat. Pinhead kept the path clear along one side of the stream, cutting away fallen branches from the winter storms.

The only sounds were the gurgling of the stream as it passed over rocks, occasional gusts of wind in the poplars and hemlocks, and the twittering of birds. The highway was too far away for traffic sounds to reach her.

Damon was her silent companion, several paces behind, invisible. She could sense him.

She got to the waterfall, her favorite place, sat on a rock, and pulled off her sneakers. She soaked her emaciated feet in the cold water and watched the flow.

The water fell over a slate ledge and dropped five feet into a wide pool. Madison remembered playing under the waterfall last summer and wishing the pool was deep enough that she could swim.

"Isn't this beautiful?" she said.

Damon phased into sight. "I've seen better."

"Just smell that air. It makes me feel healthy just smelling it."

He poked at an overhanging branch with the tip of his sword. "Can't smell it. My nose is just decoration, and I speak by magic. No lungs, remember?"

She looked up at his face, trying to read it. "I'm sorry. I didn't think."

"No problem." He slid his sword back into its sheath. "You don't mind me coming up here with you?"

"No. Should I?"

"This looked like a favorite spot for you. I wouldn't have been surprised if you had yelled at me to leave."

"I would never yell at you, Damon. You saved me when I was in the mountain."

"Oh, please. Something would have happened to snap you out of it, and you would have come flitting home just fine without me."

"No. I was gone for good, I think."

"I see that the path continues up past the falls."

"Only a little way. I can't go beyond the falls. My magic fails. Pinhead can go up and harvest wood; he seems to carry magic with him."

Damon climbed up the path that led beyond the falls, and Madison slipped her sneakers back on and followed him until they stood above the falls.

It was a small waterfall, but it was a different perspective than she usually had, and the sight captivated her. She rubbed her fingers together, and magic gathered on them. "That's not right," she said. "Up here I shouldn't be able to call up any magic, and further up I should start feeling bad. The magic is extending further than it should. Something has changed, all right."

Damon lifted his hand and examined it. "And if I go beyond the magic, I start to lose my form."

Madison poked him in the shoulder. "You're still pretty solid."

143

He looked upstream to where the wandering brook came out of the woods. "We could go further, but I suggest we don't. It wouldn't be good for either of us."

"Then just hush and let me look for a few minutes." Her legs felt tired, and she leaned on his arm. "Do you mind?"

"Better than me having to pick you up and carry you back."

There was only the rush of the stream to fill the silence. Beyond the tavern she could see Mount Majestic, rising up over the countryside like a brooding sentinel, trees dense between dark ridges. She tried to remember a time when she played with Uncle Roddyn as a child, but she couldn't. She did remember playing with Nanny last summer, and making snow monsters in winter, and how beautiful the inside of the tavern looked with all the lights up.

Tomorrow I'll be better. My hair will be darker, and I'll have flesh on my bones, and I'll look like Madison again. Then I'll have to figure out what to do about Sheriff Gazzio, and Penny, and Uncle Roddyn. But I'll be healthy tomorrow, and it will be easier for me to deal with it.

She did not know that tomorrow would be her last day on Earth.

Chapter Fourteen

She had plans when she went to bed. She would wake up earlier than usual, hide behind the door, and when Nanny came into wake her, she would shout "Boo!" She wondered if Nanny would jump, or fall to pieces, or get mad. But Madison was still sound asleep when Nanny pulled back the curtains. "Nanny!" she complained. "Couldn't you let me sleep in?"

"The early bird catches the worm, dear."

"Not if the worm is armed and dangerous." Madison rubbed her eyes, and looked over towards the window without lifting her head. It was cloudy outside.

"Are you going to float there forever, or land and start the day?"

"Huh?" She looked down and saw that she was still hovering over the quilt. That was when she dropped. "Oof!"

"You're getting better at floating, dear."

"Maybe you're getting gentler at waking me up. No, that couldn't be it." She rolled off of the bed and stretched. Her arms looked like normal arms, and her hands didn't look like cadaver hands. She hurried into Pinhead's bathroom and looked at herself in the mirror.

The tips of her hair were white, but the rest of it was now her usual dark brown hair, and it had begun to wave and frizz in its independent style. She smiled a fetching smile and tilted her head, admiring her reflection. "Nanny, I look pretty good today."

145

"You're almost beautiful, dear."

"Ha. Ha. Very funny. I'm going to get a complex and turn to a life of crime." She ran to her own bedroom and got into her work clothes.

As she hauled the garbage out to the highway, she sniffed the air. It didn't smell like rain, but she could see clouds grazing the top of Mount Majestic. It might be a cold front coming in. She knew about weather fronts.

And I know about geology first-hand, I do. I went on a field trip! I should get extra credit.

She showered, crème rinsed, and put on clean pants and a t-shirt that said "I am not a brat! I'm not! I'm not! I'm not!"

When I get a figure, I'm going to stop being a walking billboard. Maybe.

Mitch and Penny had arrived early, and were now cleaning the bar and replenishing the stock. As Madison set out her notebook and textbook – only one more chapter to go – Sheriff Carson walked in the front door.

Madison froze. Would he arrest her or something?

He ignored her, and sat down at the bar.

"Can I get you anything?" asked Mitch. "We're not really open yet."

"No, thanks, I just wanted to stop by. My vacation's over, and it seems my replacement got himself in a lot of trouble."

"Really?" Mitch polished a clean glass and hung it up on the rack.

"Seems he and this lady officer from the state police got some warrants for a local young lady, and they claimed that they picked her up but that she vanished from the back seat while they were driving down the highway. Biggest bunch of baloney you ever heard, and then they began making accusations against each other. It got embarrassing. He's been reassigned out west, and she's not answering questions anymore."

"You don't say?" Mitch had the bartender's patter down perfect.

146

"Yes, and the judge quashed the warrants, and the search has been called off. So if you see anyone that looks like a young lady with brown hair around here," he kept his gaze towards the back of the bar, "don't bother calling me. I'm not interested."

"If I see someone like that, I'll ignore her completely."

The sheriff patted the bar and stood up. He went to the front door, paused, and looked back at Mitch. "I have to admit, though. I'm curious just what went on in that car that got them both so upset."

Mitch smiled back at him.

Sheriff Carson shrugged, and left.

Madison exhaled. The magic worked, or the cooperation between the universes, whatever it was. She was safe again.

And Uncle Roddyn did nothing about it. Isn't he ever going to get better?

She put down her ball point pen and closed her notebook. She ought to go into his room and see how he was doing; she had been so concerned about herself that she hadn't talked to him lately.

She walked past the bar and down the hallway, trying to brush aside a sense of foreboding. After all, this was just her uncle. His room was dark, so she knocked on the doorway. "Uncle Roddyn?"

"Madison?" His voice was deep and raspy, as though he had a cold. "Stay out one moment. I wasn't expecting anyone." She heard a rustling of cloth. "Okay, you can step in. Don't turn on the lights, please."

She stepped inside, and as her eyes adjusted she saw a figure wrapped in a robe with the hood pulled over its head.

Why has Uncle Roddyn covered himself up?

The Rat Witch's staff lay on his lap. She realized that she never saw him anymore without the staff. "I was just seeing if you were doing okay."

"I'm fine. You needn't be concerned about me. I've just been doing a lot of thinking lately."

147

"Thinking?"

The figure shifted. "About what we're doing here. You and I, almost getting killed. Keeping the lid on the other universe. I think we've been wrong about things."

"What do you mean, wrong?" She remained standing at the door. He hadn't invited her in any further, and she didn't feel a good spirit in the room.

"This world is cramping the pocket universe," he said, "and the pocket universe wants to expand. Their worlds, Madison, are like specks inside foam bubbles, like frog eggs, and none of the billions of creatures on their millions of worlds can look up into a sky with stars and moons and distant galaxies the way we do. We've been selfishly trying to preserve our own dust speck of a world, but the little universe is destined to expand no matter what we do."

"But there's a balance. People live okay on those worlds inside, they're not suffering. There's supposed to be a balance."

"A balance? Yes, that's the story that we tell ourselves, the excuse for our actions. But at what cost? We devote our lives to that sacred Balance, and yet no one can explain why. We keep the planet called Earth safe, but not a word of thanks from earthlings, no, they bring the law down upon us, and the Escaped injure us, and what reward do we get?"

She tucked her hands behind her back and shifted her feet. She didn't want to talk about such things. She just wanted her Uncle Roddyn to be okay.

"We push them back," he continued, his voice more forceful, "the Escaped, we force them back if they don't seem useful to us, but without regard to their own worlds. All creatures deserve to grow up in their own world, to grow up among their own kind."

The figure shifted again, and a fold of the robe moved. It exposed the hand that held the Rat Witch's staff.

The fingers were scaled, and ended in claws.

Uncle Roddyn has gone back! He's reverted!

148

A sickening feeling grew in the pit of her stomach. The Caretaker had fallen, had lost his vision. Nashashuk's lightning had damaged more than Roddyn's body. It had crushed his sense of purpose. "You rest, Uncle Roddyn. You'll feel better."

"Yes, of course. Rest. Don't trouble yourself, Madison. Go enjoy yourself. Take the day off. It will all be over soon."

She stepped back a step, and another, and backed out of the room without saying goodbye.

Panic filled her, and she dashed out the door to find Nanny. She wasn't in her shed, and she wasn't in the orchard. Madison ran upstairs and found Nanny making Pinhead's bed with fresh sheets. "Nanny, oh, Nanny, Uncle Roddyn's changed, he's reverted, he's going to ruin everything...." She let the tears go that she had saved while hunting for her.

"Now, now," said Nanny, hugging Madison as she dissolved into shaking sobs, "Everything will be okay. It will work out."

"No, it won't!" Madison wailed. She struggled to quiet her voice in case Uncle Roddyn was listening. "He's got scales and claws, and he's not going to maintain the balance, he's going to let the pocket universe expand!"

Others were listening. Damon phased into visibility, and Mitch and Penny stood in the doorway. Behind them swayed Pinhead, his finger in his mouth.

"It will work out," said Nanny Bee, "but we might have to do all that we can."

"This is about that thing in the alternate cellar, right?" asked Penny. "The bright glowing thing?"

Nanny nodded. "Be very careful, all of you. Roddyn is no longer what you knew. He's a different creature entirely now, not human and very dangerous."

"But he was the Caretaker," sobbed Madison. "What will happen now? What will we do?"

"No, dear one, Roddyn was never the Caretaker."

"Of course he was. We all called him that."

149

"Only you, dear. He was never the Caretaker. He just served the part because it suited the moment."

"Then who…" Madison's eyes grew round. "You! Nanny!" She stared at her perfect face. "You're the Caretaker! You've been here forever, and you always know what to do. But why…?"

"No, dear. I am not the Caretaker either. I'm just a maid, just a helper."

"But…but who…?"

"You, dear one." She touched Madison's cheek with her cold fingertips. "Madison, you are, and have always been, the Caretaker."

"But I can't be! I'm only fourteen!" she wailed. "I can't do anything!"

"You drove back the living tree, and you defeated Nashashuk. You restored the Balance when it was slipping."

"No, I was almost killed! It was the tree that took Nashashuk, and you opened the door to the cellar, it wasn't me."

Nanny looked carefully into Madison's eyes. "And who put the tree out in the darkness, where it would be needed?"

"But, but that was an accident!"

"Nothing happens by accident, dear. Do you think Mitch and Penny coming here was just an accident? Do you think that the tree woke up after all these years, just by accident? You are the Caretaker, Madison, and although you might not feel like a great warrior, you have it within you to survive. *You* are not here by accident."

"But I almost died in the volcano, I almost vanished!"

"And who saved you? Don't preen, Damon, it doesn't become you." Nanny pulled a tissue and handed it to Madison. "Do you think it was by accident that Damon was drawn to you, so that he could find you in the heart of the mountain when no one else in this world could?"

Madison blew her nose.

My snot glands are working just fine, thank you.

150

"But what if I don't WANT to be the Caretaker?"

"Oh, dear one, we can refuse our purpose, but it leads to no good end." Nanny wrapped her arms around Madison. "I fear for you, my little girl. I saw Nashashuk when he fell the first time into the pocket universe…"

"You! You were the medicine woman! The one Étienne said lived by the pocket universe after he died!"

"No, but I was there, helping her. Much happened after that, and when you were born, I was there for you also. I gave you your first bath and I have tended you ever since." Her cold arms tightened around her. "I love you, Madison, and I fear for what is to come, because now you must stand between the two universes and save them both, and I do not know how you will do it, and I do not know how terrible the cost may be."

"Love?" asked Damon. "My good wind-up lady, how can you love?"

Nanny let go of Madison. "All beings must learn to love, Damon, even we who are second-hand creatures."

"Something heavy just walked out the back door," said Mitch, looking down the stairs.

"Be brave, Madison," said Nanny Bee. "Your time has come."

"Now?" She looked around the room, and all eyes were upon her.

Nanny Bee nodded. "You've got to stop him. You are the Caretaker." Through the window, they could hear the sound of the outside cellar door opening. "Courage, little one. You won't be alone."

Madison swallowed.

Now?

Jeans and sneakers and a t-shirt. Not very good armor against Uncle Roddyn….against the Beast.

She stumbled through the group and walked down the stairs.

Chapter Fifteen

The wind picked up and dark clouds scudded by overhead, a solid mass blocking the sunlight. Madison stepped out onto the grass and saw the creature that had been her Uncle Roddyn standing in front of the open cellar. From within came the glow of the pocket universe.

Roddyn now stood on two thick reptilian legs, and his body and short tail were covered with dense overlapping scales, dull as green iron. His head had lengthened, developing a muzzle, and his mustache had become two fleshy tentacles, like the face of a Chinese dragon. He had grown also, now twice as tall as Madison. In his claws, he grasped the Rat Witch's staff. "Be patient, Madison," he rasped when he saw her, his voice deeper than a lion's cough. "Your end will come soon enough."

"Don't do this," she pleaded. "You're a good man, Uncle Roddyn. You would never do something like this. I could always count on you."

"I was never a man!" he snarled. "I was an imitation, and I tried to please my adopted parents, but they are dead and I have nothing. I can at least free these worlds before I die."

"But you won't be freeing them! You'll be destroying them! You'll disrupt everything, and you'll destroy this earth."

"You need to break some eggs and so forth," he rasped. "In the end, it will be for the good."

Madison gathered magic into her hands. "Couldn't we talk this over for a while? I'm sure you'll change your mind."

"No." Roddyn turned away from her and thrust the staff down the stairs. He twisted it and pulled. The bright golden surface of the pocket universe bulged up from the cellar.

"Sleep!" Madison commanded, and hurled her magic at him, a bright wave, but Roddyn brushed it aside. He turned to Madison and a stream of flame shot from his mouth.

She put up both hands and made a shield, and the flames deflected away from her harmlessly.

He's turned into Godzilla! Except Godzilla was cute and rubbery, and Uncle Roddyn has become cruel and deadly.

She quickly hurled two sleep spells at Roddyn, powerful spells, but he had no problem deflecting them. He pointed the staff at her, and shot not only flames from his mouth but a bright red burst of energy from the staff. It was all she could do to shield herself.

Nanny Bee stood outside the back door of the tavern, with Damon beside her. Behind them, Penny peeked through the door.

Roddyn shoved his staff back into the surface of the golden universe, and it began to expand again.

What can I do to stop him? What is the key? If I'm the Caretaker, how am I supposed to deal with a creature like this?

She didn't know a lot of spells. Getting Escaped creatures to speak, and causing them to sleep was usually enough to handle whatever came from the little universe. Uncle Roddyn was also good at both those spells, but that meant that her spells had no chance of getting through to him.

Where is an angry tree when you need one?

Damon drew his sword and stepped away from Nanny, his eyes appraising the beast.

Is that the key, having Damon slaying the beast? His good side seems to be winning out at the moment.

She needed something. She was losing.

Then Damon, the handsome prince, yelled and charged. He got close enough to hit the beast on the back with the edge of his sword, and then he was thrown backwards by a bolt of red energy.

Madison threw a cushion of magic around Damon and he landed safely on his back. "Stay back, hollow man!" roared Roddyn, shaking the staff at him.

She ran to Damon. "Are you okay? That was brave of you!"

He struggled to his feet, his cape bearing scorch marks and his face a of disgust. "No, that was stupid of me. Look, I even dented my sword. I'm worthless." He held up Dragon's Bane, and there was a warp in the shiny blade half-way down. "His scales are like iron. Harder than iron."

Roddyn twisted the staff again, and from within the tavern came the sound of breaking wood.

"He's unleashing that thing," said Damon. "It's expanding. What are we going to do?"

Pinhead jumped out of the door of the tavern and ran towards them, followed by the slow-moving Nanny Bee. Pinhead now wore the white lab coat with the pens in the pocket; Nanny must have put them on him. The fake glasses were perched on his face, and he clutched the wild wig to his head. "Madison!" he cried. "You've got to stop him! If that pocket universe breaks loose, it will destroy this world and everyone on it!"

Behind him, Mitch stepped out of the doorway with the shotgun in his hands. He took aim at Roddyn and fired both barrels.

Roddyn roared and staggered, and then spat a stream of fire back at Mitch. Madison barely threw a shield of magic around the biker in time to save his life. The doorway of the tavern burst into flames.

Roddyn was unharmed by the buckshot. He thrust the staff back into the glowing surface and twisted it again.

"Stop him?" Madison shouted at Pinhead. "How? Pinhead, how can I stop him?"

"You've got the weapon right there!" Pinhead jabbed a finger at the sword that Damon carried.

"But it's worthless," said Damon. "Look, it's dented!"

154

The tavern roof ruptured as a loop of golden light burst through. Mitch and Penny ran towards the orchard, their hands over their heads. Debris rained down upon them, torn plywood and ripped shingles.

"You've got to become whole!" cried Pinhead, and he pulled off the wig and fell to his knees in pain.

Damon turned anguished eyes towards Madison. "How? Madison, how do I make the choice? How do I become a whole person?"

The ground lurched and she staggered. An arc of the unweaving pocket universe chewed its way through the fishing stream, hurling dirt and water into the air. Wind pummeled her, and the uncoiling strands of the little universe sounded like a hundred chainsaws as they ripped into the surroundings.

Why me, oh, why me? All I want to do is my chores and my homework and to dance with someone now and then...

No. That's weakness! Concentrate, you silly girl! How do I convince Damon that choosing the good, committing to the good, is in his best interest? If he chose evil, he might be able to stop Roddyn, but then having Damon unleashed on this world could be even worse.

She fell to her knees as a loop of the pocket universe shot up through the orchard, ripping whole trees aside.

As she struggled back to her feet, something tickled at her mind....

It was at the edge of the orchard that Watseka had appeared....

That's it!

That's it!

"Damon!" she shouted, trying to be heard over the tumult. "I've got it! Listen! Remember Watseka? Remember Étienne?"

"The two ghosts? So?"

"Damon, something of great value exists, even after death! Even after gold and fame and monuments and everything is gone, there is a treasure that can remain even after we die!"

155

"What? What treasure?" The wind whipped his black hair around his face.

"Love! Étienne and Watseka – do you remember how Étienne said that he felt he had to tell us his story? I think he had to come here, he had to tell his story so that *you* could hear it, and where you could see him and Watseka together after all those centuries! It was for you, not me!"

"I don't understand!"

"Nothing happens without a reason!" The ground shook, and she clutched his arm for support. "Damon, choosing to love someone is the goodest, I mean, the most good thing a person can do! It's unselfish, but it blesses us with a treasure that lasts beyond death, that lasts forever!"

Damon pressed his lips together and he frowned, mulling over Madison's words. She almost lost hope, but then she saw light dawn in Damon's eyes. "Yes." He nodded. "I do remember. And much as I hate to admit it, you are right. I believe you."

"There is no time!" screamed Pinhead, pressing the wig against his narrow skull. "Behold, the end of your world!" He pointed towards Mount Majestic.

Through the wind and dust and debris, Madison saw the distant top of Mount Majestic blow apart. Roaring thunder shook the earth as smoke and gases and glowing pumice shot from the broken peak.

Mount Majestic had awoken.

Damon whirled back to her. He pulled his sword and held it upside down, like a holy symbol. "It takes two, Madison! Do you understand what I'm saying?"

Madison stepped back and swallowed. She hadn't thought it all the way through, but now she saw it.

She saw what had to be.

I was the one he was drawn to, I was the one that he could sense even when I was just a dying spark in that bloody mountain, and I could always sense him.

The implication rocked her, and she desperately wanted more time to think things through, but Damon thrust his hands forward, the hilt gripped tightly, his coal-black eyes searching hers. "It's you that has to decide now, Madison, not me. It's you. I know what my decision is going to be, but I can't do it without you!"

Protect me, protect me, help me not to be wrong....

She drew in a shuddering breath and made her own choice. "Yes, Damon. Both of us, you and me."

"Forever?"

"Forever."

"You're a brave girl, Madison. Now put your hands on mine and hold on tight!"

Her world tilted, and as she reached out her arms and laid her hands on his hands, she felt her childhood slip away. "I will hold on, Damon. Always."

He closed his eyes. "I choose!" he said firmly. "I choose the good, and I choose love above all else!"

A brilliant flash of light enveloped them, and exploded out in all directions. Madison had to hold on with all of her might to keep from being blown away.

The light expanded in a sphere around them, and for a moment they had quiet.

Damon opened his eyes and they were blue, deep blue as though a child had colored them with a crayon. The dimple on his chin was gone, and his hair was now brown and choppy. His cape had vanished, and he wore black pants, black boots, and a simple white homespun shirt.

She was bonded to him. Thoroughly, magically, and spiritually bonded to him. As she looked at his face, she could picture their children and their children's children, a beautiful family raised in perfect love.

He breathed in deeply through his nose, and then he smiled, a peaceful smile that warmed her clear through. "You were right. The air does smell wonderful!"

She started to reply, but the moment passed and the roar and chaos returned.

"Now!" cried Pinhead. "Or it will be forever too late!"

Damon lifted his sword. The dent was gone, and a pale blue flame rippled along its edges. He spoke to it with a grim smile. "Dragon's Bane. That's the name that appeared on you when that young virgin Commanded me to be a prince. Nothing happens without a reason." He turned towards the beast called Roddyn.

Damon now has a heart and I know he does because I can feel it.

Damon swung back his sword, and Madison flung magic at it. "Be true!" she Commanded, and then Damon hurled the sword at Roddyn, the sword that had been forged from Damon's own being.

Glowing brightly and trailing magic, Dragon's Bane rotated handle over point, once, twice, three times, and then buried itself to the hilt in the beast's scaled chest.

Roddyn screamed, a roar that shattered the stone chimney and collapsed the side of the tavern. He clutched at the sword, trying to pull it out, but it vanished into smoke, leaving an open wound. When he screamed again, fire tore from his chest.

Madison grabbed Damon's hand and gripped it tightly as the beast staggered sideways, clutching at the burning wound. One more wail and the beast collapsed, shaking the ground.

"Grab the Rat Witch's staff!" shouted Pinhead. "You've got to go into the pocket universe and then pull back the space-time, wind it back on the staff!" He clutched at Madison with frantic hands. "We all need to go into the pocket universe! We have to restore the balance! It's getting worse every moment!"

"Stay close to me!" shouted Damon to Madison. Hand in hand, they ran past the body of the beast, and then Damon grabbed hold of the staff. Madison looked up and saw great glowing arcs like giant snakes twisting up into the clouds.

158

Damon turned the staff back and forth, his face thoughtful. "I understand this thing!" he shouted over the noise. "I used staves like this back when I was learning the dark arts. It's not evil of itself, but it's powerful!"

"We've got to go in!" Pinhead's face was twisted with pain, but he kept the wig pressed tightly on his head. "All of us!"

Nanny appeared, carrying Emtianal's avatar, lying limp in her arms. "Take him also," said Nanny. "It's time."

Madison lifted the avatar from Nanny's arms. It felt light, hollow. "Nanny, you're coming with us?"

She shook her head. "No, dear, I'm staying behind."

"But the Balance! You've got to come with us!"

"No." Her face crinkled into a sad smile. "I'm just a machine, Madison. It would be like tossing in rocks; I would not have any effect. But if I stay, I can be here for the next Caretaker."

"There!" shouted Damon. He had the staff thrust into the surface of the pocket universe, and a forested world was visible through the brane. "This is a good world for us! Hurry!"

"Nanny!" cried Madison. "You can't stay behind! I've never been without you!"

Nanny Bee wrapped her arms around Madison and hugged her tight, being careful of Emtianal's avatar. "Oh, dear heart, I know, and I love you so, but your destiny lies there, and mine lies here, and so we must part."

"No!" sobbed Madison. It was all happening too fast.

"Remember me, dear. I will never forget you. And I envy you, that you can shed tears and I cannot."

"Nanny!" she cried one more time, but Pinhead grasped her arm and separated them.

"Go, Madison," shouted Damon. "I'll be right behind!"

Pinhead pulled at her, and she fell forwards into the brane.

Nanny!

Slowly she sank, passing through the golden boundary between her world and the pocket universe.

159

Chapter Sixteen

Holding Emtianal's avatar in her arms, Madison emerged from the rippling surface of the sky and plummeted. Beside her was Pinhead and far, far below them lay the forest, broken by tended fields and a village crossroads.

We're falling to our death!

She couldn't breathe. She kept remembering all the moments she had with Nanny and how she never understood how fleeting they were, how precious, but with desperation she pushed the thoughts aside and reached inside of herself. Somewhere deep inside was the place that let her float when she slept.

Pinhead gripped her arm, and with his other hand he clutched the gray wig as though it was a broken safety rope. From his open mouth came a high warbling scream.

There. That is the place inside me where I float. All I need to do is...

The avatar jerked in her arms, and cracked. A split appeared along the side and an enormous butterfly with a thick body pulled itself out. It perched on the broken avatar and spread its wings, marvelous green diaphanous wings that rippled in the wind.

The wind lifted it away, and Madison dropped the useless remains.

Moth-man, Damon called Emtianal. He was so much more beautiful than a moth.

She risked a glance up over her shoulder, and saw Emtianal drifting on his gossamer wings. He, at least, would be safe.

She looked down and saw the ground rushing up to meet them. She concentrated deep within and called upon the place that let her float.

Float.

Their descent slowed and the wind lessened. Pinhead clung to her, his eyes white with fear, and she extended her magic to include him.

I didn't know I could do that. But I'm in a different world now. I don't know what I can do.

Nanny.

The crushing pain of their separation returned, as she knew it would again and again. How could she go on without ever seeing Nanny again? Who would wake her up and make her be sensible?

And what had happened to Damon? She looked up but she couldn't see him. She could sense, him, though, somewhere above her.

What happened between us? I can feel him clear as anything, and it's not like we are just friends, it's like we each have become a half of a unity. I didn't expect to form a bond with him like that, but I guess it was the only way to transform him. And we didn't even go out for a burger or dance or anything! I haven't even kissed him yet!

They were plummeting again, so she looked down and concentrated, slowing their descent. She aimed for the crossroads that lay below them. Pinhead stopped screaming and shoved his finger in his mouth.

She could see many huts on one side of the crossroads, and plowed fields on the other. Gently they descended, and their feet settled upon the packed dirt road as if they had stepped from a curb.

Pinhead plopped down on the road, the wig in his lap. "Are we done falling?" he asked, looking up at her.

"Yes, Pinhead. We're safe."

"I was scared. Why are you crying?"

161

"Because I miss Nanny."

"Oh." He looked around. "I don't know where she is."

"She's far away, Pinhead." She almost said, *and we'll never see her again*, but she didn't want to make Pinhead cry also.

"I don't know where we are. We're lost."

"No, we're not lost, we're just in a different place. Damon said it was a good world, so we'll be safe."

I hope.

Villagers ran towards them, coming out of the crude buildings with grass roofs, short villagers, jabbering and pointing at them.

Madison looked up at the sky and searched for Damon, but she couldn't see him. The sky was so different from Earth's sky – she could see ripples in it, moving like slow waves on the sea. The light came from a certain direction, casting shadows, but there was not a separate sun.

These worlds are so different than mine. It could take me forever just to figure out how the light can work if there aren't suns and stars. Things probably operate by magic here.

She wondered if it ever rained, and if there were seasons. Now that she was here, she would find out first-hand.

She became aware of the surrounding crowd. They looked like children, but with faces that were adult and almost animal-like.

We've attracted some attention, it seems. I wonder if this is the world that the Rat Witch came from? They look similar.

A troop of men arrived with pitchforks and axes, the leader shouting in a strange language and pointing in her direction.

That looks like trouble. Let's hope my spells work.

Madison flicked a Common Tongue spell in all directions, and the crowd fell back in a wave, many of them tossed flat on their backs.

I better back off a bit next time. My magic seems to be pretty powerful in this world.

She rubbed her fingertips together, and felt magic gather on them like a film of honey.

"She's another of them witches," said one of the men, shaking his pitchfork as he lay on the ground.

"Tie her up and send her out to sea!" shouted a fat woman.

She wafted comforting and calming magic in their direction and they quieted. They climbed to their feet, dusted each other off and looked in her direction with concern. The leader of the troop of men pulled his cloth hat from his head and inched towards her, tugging nervously at his long beard. "Oh, great woman from, um," he swallowed, "from the sky, please don't hurt us."

Madison smiled at him, hoping it would be a reassuring smile. "Don't be afraid. I won't hurt anyone."

A woman in a dark orange dress and braided brown hair walked up beside the man with the long beard. She squinted at Pinhead, who still had his finger in his mouth, and then at Madison. "What are you? What are you doing here?"

What should I say? I guess I'm going to be here for a while, maybe forever. I need to start out right with them.

"My name is Madison."

She heard them say her name and then turn and repeat it to the people behind them, who in turn passed her name to the people behind them.

And I'm here to what? Conquer and rule? Find a place to hide?

She looked at the fields, and remembered what she had learned about agriculture. Their soil was thin and eroded because the furrows were straight instead of contoured. She could teach them how to make their fields more fertile, how to rotate their crops, how to breed better producing grains.

She gasped.

I remember everything! I remember all my notebooks, every single one, and all the math and literature and biology and everything that I ever studied!

And I remember...

Oh! Oh, dear merciful, merciful heaven! I remember!

163

She could remember her father playing catch with her and showing her how to fish. She remembered the buggies pulling up to the side of the old tavern, and the lovely horses that she not only touched but that she got to sit on and ride. Tears flowed once more, because she could remember her mother singing to her. She recalled how her mother would hug her and tuck her in bed, exactly how she looked and exactly how her voice sounded.

She even remembered the last day when her mother's age-spotted hand could only touch her on the head, and then the funeral and the burial that she couldn't attend because she couldn't leave the tavern without getting ill.

She hugged herself with bittersweet joy.

"Why are you crying?" the short woman asked.

"Because," answered Madison, when she was able to speak, "because I remember my mother and father."

"She came from the sky," whispered the man with the braided beard to an old man behind him, "and she's crying because she remembers her mother and father."

"Maybe she got lost," the old man whispered back.

"Why are you here?" asked the short woman again.

Madison wiped her eyes and lifted her head. She looked at the poor fields and the ragged huts. The people in front of her were wearing badly made clothes and rags. "I am here to teach," she said.

"I see," said the woman. She bowed.

Madison looked up at the sky, and there was still no sign of Damon, yet she could feel him up there, almost as though he was frozen. "Pinhead, could you put the wig on one more time and tell me when Damon will land?"

Pinhead climbed to his feet and the people fell back, some pressing against the split rail fence. Pinhead was indeed startling at first sight. "Put on the wig?"

"One more time, please."

"Okay. It hurts." Pinhead pushed the wig on top of his narrow head, and his eyes focused. "You wish to know when

164

Damon will land on this world? Right now, he is winding in the space-time that Roddyn let loose with the staff. He is re-creating the Balance. For Damon, that will take less than an hour, and then he will descend."

"For Damon. Will it be different for me?"

"Yes." A tear rolled down Pinhead's cheek. "Time runs faster down here on this world, and you are now aging like everyone else here. So for you, Damon will land on this world in ninety....in ninety two...."

"Minutes? Ninety two minutes?"

Pinhead didn't answer but only ground his teeth in pain.

"Please, Pinhead! He'll land in ninety two hours? Certainly not in ninety two days? Tell me!"

"He will be down in...ninety...two...years...."

Madison gasped in horror. "Ninety two years? Are you sure?"

"Yes!" cried Pinhead. "He will be down in Ninety! Two! Years!" He ripped the wig off and threw it at Madison's feet. He pulled off the white coat and glasses, dropped them on top of the wig, and then he lay down in the weeds by the fence and covered his head with his hands.

"Ninety two years." Madison staggered over to the fence and grasped it, trying not to fall down. Her prince, her other half, Damon – she had not thought of him as her beloved, but that was what he had suddenly become – It would be over ninety years before he landed.

"I'm only fourteen," she whispered to no one, her fingers in front of her lips. "But I'll be....I'll be what? A hundred and six when he lands? I won't live that long. I can't, if I'm aging normally now."

She turned around, and stared at the crowd of villagers gathered in a semicircle around her.

I don't have Nanny, and I don't have Uncle Roddyn – he's dead – and I don't have Emtianal, I think, or even Mitch or Penny. And now I won't have Damon.

She looked at Pinhead, who lay sobbing in the weeds at her feet. How long would he last? She had no idea, but he was hardly a companion.

She was alone.

The whispering and buzzing of the crowd caught her attention. The people in front were telling the latecomers behind them about the Great Teacher, the woman who flew down from the sky, and the strange giant that came down with her.

They're like munchkins. I'm surrounded by munchkins.

Someone began shrieking and pushing through the crowd. "Gives me back my staff, you sneaky thief!"

Oh, no. The Rat Witch.

The little creature, in a loose purple robe, pushed aside two villagers and stood in front of Madison. "I wants my staff back! Gives it to me now!"

"I can't do that," said Madison. "It's being used by Damon to heal the sky."

"What? What? What's a Damon?" The Rat Witch looked up, jerking her head back and forth as she studied the sky.

"He's my beloved, but he won't land down here until..." She struggled to keep speaking. "...until ninety two years from now."

"But my staff! I wants my staff!" The Rat Witch spun in place and stared at the sky again. "Thiefs! You are both Thiefs!" She shook her small brown fist at the sky, shrieked, and ran back through the crowd. Madison watched her until the little creature hopped into the air and vanished.

She took a deep shuddering breath and tried to decide what to do next. There would be time for her to wallow in self-pity later. Time enough for her to live in her past memories, and think about all the might-have-beens, and to mourn for what would never be.

Her memory was good, her memory was complete, in this world, but that would be a mixed blessing.

She had been the Caretaker. How could she have forgotten that, when she lived back at the tavern? And as Caretaker, if she could no longer protect the balance between the two universes, she could at least do good in this world and bring what knowledge and blessings she could to these little people. She could teach them how to live better, how to be healthy, even how to govern themselves wisely and how to love each other.

I will be their Great Teacher from the sky, and if heaven is kind, maybe I will live long enough to say goodbye to Damon before I die.

She took one last woeful look at the sky, and then reached down and lifted Pinhead to his feet. She gathered up the wig, and the glasses, and the lab coat.

Then she learned the names of the leaders, and went with them to their village to start her new life.

Mitch McKenzie wiped non-existent spots from the new black quartz bar top and beamed with pride. "Don't it look fine? I tell you, that old top was all stained and worn out."

"Eh." Penny looked up from setting out napkin holders on the new white tablecloths. "Nobody ever noticed. It was just part of the flavor of the old tavern."

"Maybe, but this looks so much better. Tomorrow should be a big crowd here, especially with the Jug and Fiddle band coming to play."

"Eh."

"There's still time to change the name, you know."

"No, I like 'The Padded Cell.' It's one of the things that attracted me to it. Imagine if this place was called 'Mountain View Tavern' or something. I would have driven right on by."

Mitch tossed the rag to Nanny, who was too slow to catch it. "What do you think, Nanny? Keep it 'The Padded Cell?'"

Nanny picked up the rag from the floor and stuffed it into the laundry bag. The kitchen was clean and ready to go. The hairy-armed cook now had an assistant, a graying butter-ball of a man who had demonstrated a minestrone soup seasoned to perfection. Customers would probably complain that the soup never tasted as good as Madison made it, but Madison was gone for good and soon they would forget.

But Nanny would not forget, not ever. She had gathered together what notebooks of Madison had survived the holocaust and sealed them away in the back of the new storage room. "I think Madison would have wanted us to keep the name," she said.

Mitch frowned. "I can't believe it's been months since she fell into a different world and that she won't come back. I keep feeling like any moment she'll come charging down those steps again. Do you think she's okay?"

"Time runs differently there," said Nanny. "She might have already lived a lifetime of adventure. I hope so. Madison could never live a quiet life. But we'll never know."

The reconstructed tavern had a wine cellar, of course, which stocked more than wine. As before, the letters that said WINE CELLAR could be slid to one side, causing the pocket universe to become visible. The golden little universe was small and quiet, and during the months of reconstruction nothing had Escaped. The Balance was restored, and it would be many years before creatures might Escape again.

Mount Majestic had gone back to sleep. Everyone from the disaster teams blamed the damage on the unexpected eruption; many farm houses were demolished, and disaster relief had poured in from the federal and state agencies. Mitch and Penny were able to reconstruct The Padded Cell without incurring large debts.

Mitch and Penny had gotten married right after the eruption, and then pitched in to rebuild. Uncle Roddyn's disappearance had left them as full owners, and they never told anyone about his transformation. Mitch called in favors from a couple of friends, who used cables and heavy equipment to drag the dead beast away from the tavern and to bury the body beyond the fishing stream. "You got a choice," said Mitch. "Keep quiet and enjoy free drinks for a month, or you can tell people about this and you'll never know for sure what's in your glass."

His friends kept quiet.

Penny sat down, ran her fingers through her garish red hair, and exhaled. "I don't know where my energy has gone, lately. I keep having to sit."

Nanny put her laundry bag down at the back door. "You should rest often, Mrs. McKenzie, especially in your condition."

"Please, Nanny, just call me....what do you mean, my condition?"

"You're expecting. You should take it easy."

"But..." Penny looked puzzled. "How did you know? I mean, I'm not showing or anything. In fact, I just found out myself."

Nanny nodded. "I am very good at sensing physiological changes. I could tell."

"But it don't make sense to me," said Mitch. "I've been to a doctor, and I can't have any kids. I don't understand how she's expecting."

"It's the magic of the two universes," said Nanny. "A Caretaker is always needed, and when the old Caretaker leaves, a new one is brought forth. I expected this to happen."

Mitch scratched his head. "But...am I...?"

"Yes, you are the father. Absolutely. She will need both of you. Have you thought of a name for her yet?"

Penny raised her eyebrows. "Her?"

"Yes, her." Nanny's perfect face crinkled into a smile. "The Caretaker is always a girl."

Chapter Seventeen

The Great One's bearers walked carefully up the cobbled pathway to the Hallowed Field, and her nurse walked alongside. It was a great honor to carry the Sky Princess, the Queen, the Great Teacher, she who was known by many names, and they were among the select few who knew her by her real name, Madison.

She lay upon the litter, her hand upon her chest, keeping her heart beating and her lungs breathing with her magic. The decades had passed slowly, but they had eventually passed, and the day had arrived when the legendary Damon would land as foretold with exactness by Pinhead the Gardener before he passed on.

Pinhead had settled into gardening in a little hut by the village, growing marvelous vegetables and flowers that were the legend of the continent. People visited from far countries to watch and learn as he tended his beds. He had lived many years, and died peacefully among friends.

Emtianal had visited Madison in his butterfly form, but he could not speak without his avatar. He would drift in during occasions and perch on the back of her chair, or beside her, sipping a juice with his proboscis while people passed by and gazed at him in awe. Then he would take wing and silently fly away. He only appeared in the summers, and after several years he was never seen again.

The bearers stopped in the center of the Hallowed Field, and rested Madison's litter on the ground. They scanned the sky, looking for a sign. "There!" a woman cried, and they all looked to where she was pointing.

Madison looked up and saw a figure descending, but she already knew where Damon was without even seeing him; she had always felt his presence. He clung to a staff which pulled down a cone from the sky, a funnel-shaped surface wavering like a pale blue tornado.

One of the bearers, a tall woman named Richelle, knelt beside Madison. "We can see him, Great One!" she said. "I can't believe this is actually happening! The Healer of the Sky comes to earth and we are here to see him, just like it was prophesied!"

"Remember.... what I've taught you... let him speak first... and keep the people... back..." Madison could only utter a short phrase at a time, using her magic to pull each breath into her ancient lungs. On the other side of the litter, her scribe scratched away, recording everything.

"We will keep them back, Great One," said Richelle. "You will have all the time you need to speak with him before the people celebrate."

"Thank you..."

Damon descended faster and faster as he joined with the time of this particular world, and Madison spared a touch of magic to cushion his landing. She turned her head to the side and saw thousands of people, some small, some tall, circling the Hallowed Field, dressed in their colorful finest and holding their children aloft so that they might see.

The prince landed at the center of the Hallowed Field, precisely where Pinhead had predicted. The people sighed and cheered, holding themselves back only because the Great Teacher had requested it.

Welcome home, Beloved. I hope you are not horrified by the withered old woman who awaits you.

Madison watched Damon turn about in a circle, his face confused. Richelle stepped forward and bowed, catching his attention. He nodded at her and asked, "Where did all these people come from? Am I interrupting something?"

Richelle straightened but kept her eyes down. "They are gathered here to await your coming, Oh Great One, Healer of the Sky."

Damon leaned on his staff, the Rat Witch's staff with which he had pulled the pocket universe back into balance. The staff's emerald glowed a brilliant green and throbbed with power. "Really? How odd. That's all well and good, and I appreciate it, but I want to see Madison first."

Richelle gasped and bowed again by reflex.

She heard my real name from his lips. No wonder she's flustered.

"This way," Richelle said, gesturing with a trembling hand towards where Madison lay. Damon picked up the staff and walked towards the litter, his eyes scanning the crowd.

Look at him. Those brilliant blue eyes, the white shirt, the choppy brown hair, just as I saw him so many decades ago when we parted. So young, so confident. Maybe I shouldn't let him know it's me.

Damon looked at her without recognition. "Pardon me, old one," he said respectfully, kneeling beside her litter. "Could you please tell me where Madison is? She's a young girl that would have landed here just a few minutes ago."

"Damon... I have... bad news...."

His face fell, and he gripped the staff tightly. "She's hurt?"

"No, you.... dear boy. It's me...."

"You?" He moved closer, looking into her eyes. "Madison? Is that you?"

She nodded, with great effort.

172

He looked at her withered arms, her white hair, and her bony face. "What happened to you?" he whispered.

"I got old... while you were.... healing the sky... decades passed.... down here..."

"But it was just a short while, only minutes!"

"Time moves.... differently.... on these worlds."

"Oh, Madison. I am so sorry." He reached out to grasp her hand, which lay upon her chest.

"Not that hand... please....."

Her nurse, a thin dark woman, knelt beside them. "The Great One is keeping herself alive with magic," she said quietly to Damon. "You must not take away that hand." She lifted Madison's other hand from the cot and laid it gently into Damon's palm. "Don't squeeze. Her bones break easily."

Damon forced a smile as he looked at Madison again. "We have the worst luck, you and I."

"We paid... the price... to save these... worlds...."

"But our time together is so suddenly gone. If only I'd known."

"We will have.... all the time... we need.... after you come.... to join me.... in the world.... beyond..."

He rested his other hand on top of hers. She felt the warmth from his palms, and realized that she must feel cold to him. "I pray that will be soon," he said.

"No, Damon... you must live.... a long life... you have... only now become.... what you were.... meant to be..."

"I am only what you made me, Madison. I was two broken creatures that wouldn't fit together. You had faith in me, and you were the key that made me whole. You made me human again, and now I have a heart, and I can love." He smiled and patted his chest. "And I can breathe! All my parts work again."

"Goodness.... Richelle... the Healer of the... Sky must be... thirsty..."

Richelle put her hand to her mouth. "Oh! I forgot!" She turned and gestured. "Cup-bearer!"

173

A short woman with her hair in braids stepped forward. Her brown dress was threaded with gold, and she held a golden goblet with both hands. Her brow furrowed in concentration as she held the cup out to the prince, and she said, "For you, Oh Healer of the Sky, it's from...." Her eyes widened with panic, and then she finished rapidly, "...a cold pure spring in the mountains."

Damon rose to his feet, towering over her. He took the cup and sipped from it, smiled, and then drank it down completely. He exhaled and handed the cup back to her. "Thank you," he said, looking into the short woman's eyes. "That was delicious."

The woman fainted.

Madison refrained from laughing out loud. She could break a rib if she wasn't careful. Damon looked at her, puzzlement on his face, and she said, "You can't.... blame them... Damon... you're like a.... rock star.... to them."

"I'll try not to smile at them, then, if it's going to make them keel over. Madison, what happened all this time? What have you been doing?"

"My scribe...can tell you...everything...."

"Scribe?"

"Everything... I have ever.... said or done.... has been... written down... I fear.... my library... is quite tedious.... Now, look... across the valley... Damon... The light.... is just right..."

Richelle pointed, and Damon turned and looked in that direction.

The morning light shone upon a great castle nestled against the far mountain, rich with towers and battlements. Waterfalls glistened on either side, and banners waved in the breeze.

"I'm afraid... it's a bit like... Cinderella's castle... but I built it... for you..."

Damon knelt beside her again. "It's beautiful, it's amazing, but you built it for me?"

"I remembered.... everything I studied... all those years.... nothing is by... accident." She rested a moment, gathering strength. "I taught them.... how to mine.... how to build... the

174

rooms are... very masculine... for you... I used lots.... of bold colors.... and antlers.... You will see.... some paintings... of you and me.... side by side...."

"It's magnificent, but it will be empty without you, Madison."

"I'm sorry.... Damon." She felt her heart growing feebler under her hand, and each breath became more difficult. "It was all.... I could do.... Richelle... and the other.... tall ones... I found across... the sea... a great adventure.... I have taught... her well..." She paused, then forced herself to continue. "When I'm gone.... you and her... should... have children.... you would be.... a great father...."

"Madison. I could never embrace another woman, now that I've bonded with you." He brushed a strand of white hair from her face. "I loved you when you were too young, and I love you now when you're old."

"You've never.... even kissed... me yet... I'm sorry... I'm so old..." She paused, and drew in a shuddering breath. "Oh.... please.... my magic is... almost gone... Kiss me once.... before...."

There was an explosion nearby, and someone started shrieking, shouting, and pushing their way through the crowd. Richelle stood up, her hand on the knife at her hip.

"Now..... what...?" asked Madison.

"My staff! Gives me back my staff!" cried the Rat Witch, waving her arms in a frenzy and flapping the sleeves of her purple robe. "I throws myself decades ahead, you thiefs, decades, just so I could gets my staff back, so now gives it to me!"

"What is this?" asked Damon.

"Uncle Roddyn.... took her staff... the one... you hold.... I suppose.... you could.... give it back...."

"Gives me that, you mooglit!" The Rat Witch, half the height of the prince, grabbed the staff and yanked it away from him. "It's mine! It's mine!"

"It served its purpose," said Damon calmly. "Keep it. It's yours."

"Mine!" The Rat Witch cackled and danced, holding the staff overhead. "At last, again it's mine, it's mine, mine, mine!"

Damon knelt by Madison once more. "Annoying creature," he said.

"Please.... Damon.... I have.... no life... left.... Would you....?"

"Of course, dear Madison. With all my heart." He bent over her to kiss her, but the Rat Witch began shrieking again.

"Filthy!" the Rat Witch shouted. "Look what you've done! It's gots years wrapped all around it, my staff is filthy with time! Hundreds of years! I won't stands for it!"

Madison felt her heartbeat stop.

Please, Damon, ignore her. Kiss me now before my spirit leaves.

She couldn't speak. Her magic was gone.

Her life was over.

"Thousands of years even! Takes them back!" the Rat Witch screamed, and a bright beam of red light hit Damon and knocked him away.

No!

"And you, too, you sneaky thief!" A wall of red light slammed into Madison's side and knocked her off her cot. She rolled several times and came to a stop with the cot lying over her.

Every bone in my body must be shattered. How cruel, how unfair, to ruin our last moment together, our one and only kiss.

She heard screams from the crowd, and people running. Her bearers and Richelle must be trying to defend her, but with the staff, the Rat Witch would be too powerful to overcome. Besides, the harm was done; the Great Teacher and the Healer of the Sky had been destroyed.

Or was Damon only stunned? He was young, after all; he was resilient.

The cot lay across her face, and she pushed it aside so that she could see. Where was he? Was that him lying on the ground? *How did I move that cot?*

She held her hand out in front of her face and looked at it. It was full-fleshed, and the skin was fair and pink and smooth. So was her arm.

What in the world?

She pushed herself upright, and nothing hurt. She took a deep breath, and felt her heart beating strongly in her chest.

Richelle knelt beside her, her face white with astonishment. "Great One?"

Madison pulled her feet under her, which wasn't easy. It had been many years since she had stood up, but she managed it. She looked around at the milling people, then down at Damon.

He was up on one elbow, blinking. He was alive, although a bit dusty.

She saw the people surrounding the Rat Witch, and her bearers and guardians being held back by beams of red light from the Rat Witch's staff. "Hold!" Madison cried. "Let her alone!" Her bearers turned and saw Madison standing straight and tall, and they backed away and lowered their weapons.

Madison reached down, grabbed Damon's hand, and pulled him to his feet. He looked at her with astonishment.

"Close your mouth," said Madison, suppressing a giggle. "It makes you look dull-witted!"

He closed his mouth. "Madison?"

"Yes?" She inhaled deeply and stretched her arms, amazed at the lack of pain. She had had to learn to live with pain as she aged, and the freedom of motion was marvelous.

"What happened just now? You look young!"

"The Rat Witch. The nasty little wonderful creature used us as rags to dispose of all that time you wrapped up on the staff! Look at me!" She twirled with her arms over her head, still wearing the brown dress she had worn as an old woman on a litter. "She made me fourteen again!"

177

She looked down at her body. "No! Wait!" She rubbed her fingertips together, and then clapped her hands on her head and ran them down her sides. When she took her hands away, she was dressed in a snowy white gown with a wondrously full skirt, a tight waist, a scoop neck over her bosom, and short blousy sleeves, all trimmed in blue and gold. "I didn't go back to fourteen! I look eighteen!" She curtseyed low before Damon, and then looked up with a grin on her face.

"Well, look at you," he said admiringly. "You look...almost beautiful!"

"Almost!" She punched him on the shoulder. "You beast, I am like totally gorgeous!"

He grabbed her hands and laughed out loud. "Yes, you are. The most totally gorgeous woman I have ever seen. And now I must do this."

He put his hands on the sides of her face and tilted her face up towards him. Gently, but thoroughly, he kissed her.

A sphere of white light flashed outwards from them in all directions, and she felt as though she was lifted a foot off the ground. As she tried to recover her poise, she saw that the people all around them were flat on their backs again. "I...I...I need to learn to control that." She patted his arm. "We'll need lots of practice. Lots."

"We'll have years to practice, Madison. That Rat Witch said there were hundreds of years wrapped around that staff."

At the mention of her name, the Rat Witch clapped her hands and cried, "Hee hee heee!" She turned and ran away, pushing through the crowd. "Woot!" she yelled, and disappeared.

Madison took Damon's hand and smiled radiantly. "Thousands of years, actually, is what she said. We might have a long life together, Damon. I hope you can stand me that long."

"I'll give it a try."

"Oh!" She punched his shoulder again. "And if you touch, if you even *think* of touching Richelle, I'll personally break every bone in your body!"

178

He laughed, and she realized how much she loved his laughter. "I want to see that castle you built."

"Yes! Right now!" She turned to Richelle. "Send runners to all the villages! An hour before sunset, at the castle gates, there will be a royal wedding for the Great Teacher and the Healer of the Sky!"

"Yes, Great One! Right away!" Richelle beamed and began shouting orders to the other bearers.

"A wedding? Today?" asked Damon.

"I've spent a lifetime being aware of your presence, Mister Rock Star, and I'm not going to wait one more day! Besides, I've got some redecorating to do starting tomorrow."

"Redecorating?"

"Those awful antlers have got to go! And I'll need some pastels in the dining room, and some lace in the bedrooms, and, and, but I'll check with you, Damon, I'll ask your opinions, we'll do this together!"

He smiled and nodded, his expression calm and content. Around them was orderly chaos as runners leaped on odd-looking four-legged animals and galloped off in all directions, and bells began to ring in the nearby villages. "Bells?"

"I taught them mining and metals and casting and everything. The bells were going to be for my funeral, but now they're for my wedding. Every village has them." She danced in her eagerness. "Let's go! I want to run!" She grabbed his hand. "Let's run to the castle!"

"Together," he said, gripping her hand firmly. "No racing. Side by side."

"Always," she nodded, and pulled him into a fast run.

The crowd parted and cheered as they passed, still stunned by the miracle. The Great Teacher was young again!

Madison and Damon ran swiftly away from the Hallowed Field, leaving all the celebrants behind. "You're fast!" exclaimed Damon.

"That's nothing!" she shouted. "Watch this!"

"Be careful! That's a cliff up ahead!"

Madison didn't hesitate. With a flick of her fingers, she leaped off the edge and pulled Damon with her.

They didn't fall, but rose into the air surrounded by a glow of magic. Her voluminous skirts rippled and the wind lifted and tousled Damon's hair.

"You can fly!" he shouted as they skimmed over the treetops.

"Yes, but you don't know how yet! Keep hold of my hand!"

"Forever," he said, and their eyes connected.

They sailed out over the valley, and bells began ringing as they passed, bells in all the villages, bells that tolled for the miracle of Madison reborn, bells that tolled for the Healer of the Sky, and bells that tolled for the joy of their new world.

END

Dedicated to Renée

My special thanks to Mindy Klasky, the author of more than fifteen novels in a variety of genres including the Glasswrights Series (traditional fantasy), the Jane Madison Series, and the As You Wish Series (both light paranormal romance). Many of her works are available on Amazon.com, and I recommend them. She has faithfully and diligently critiqued each of my novels, and her help is much appreciated.

Cover art by Nolan Sundrud

You would be surprised how much a review helps an author be found. If you go to http://www.amazon.com/dp/B007SQP8ZG or search Amazon for Sundrud, click on the current reviews of this book, you will be able to post your own review. Thank you!

If you enjoyed THE POCKET UNIVERSE, you will also enjoy GOLDENEYES.

Here is a bonus chapter from the novel.

GOLDENEYES

Chapter One

    I placed a smooth rock in the dirt, matching it to the other five already there, making a hexagon out of a pentagon. A hexagon felt right. I used to be five and liked pentagons, but after my birthday party I am now six, and so hexagons are best.

    I ignored the shouts of the other children playing kickball and enjoying the spring weather. There weren't many of them; the colony had only ten men and twelve women now. There had been nine children in my age group, the first children born on this planet, but one had been carried off last year. I was the oldest, the firstborn.

    The strange one.

    I brushed my white hair out of my face and looked carefully at a stone, admiring the grain of it. We were now up to seventeen children. There was just no symmetry in that at all.

    The kickball bounced off a post and rolled up against my leg. It was the inflated bladder of a new world llama with the tubes tied off. I picked it up and placed it in the center of the ring of stones, where it fit quite nicely.

    Bo Kiptanui ran up and skidded to a stop. "Don't just sit there, stupid! Throw it back!"

Bo was the second child born after the colony began. Bo had Polynesian skin and handled the bright sun almost as well as I did. He also enjoyed being the biggest.

I squinted up at him. "My name is Jia, not 'stupid,' and I'm not playing kickball."

Bo put his hands on his knees. "Stupid is your fame and Goldeneyes your name," he said in a nasal tone. "Now gimme the ball."

I picked up the kickball. "You want this ball?"

"Yes."

His aura was green, not angry red, so I could tell he was more concerned with playing than beating on me. "Then go get it." I threw the ball behind me.

Bo put his hand on my forehead and pushed me backwards, hard, then scattered my stones before he ran to get the ball. I waited until he had the ball before I sat back up. By then the others had begun the chant, "Goldeneyes, Goldeneyes, always telling stupid lies, can't spell, can't read, no one likes a half-breed!"

If Mrs. Graham had been around she would have stopped them, but she was inside the log schoolhouse so they chanted it again.

I started gathering my little stones to remake my hexagon, but when I reached out to a far stone, I saw a man-like creature out of the corner of my eye. It was standing just beyond the piece of slate that was third base.

I jumped to my feet. "Bo! Don't go near third base! There's a bad man!"

The chanting died away.

If you took a human and hunched it down, and made the skin rough and gray and the hair like strings and the eyes yellow and the teeth pointed, it would look like the creature I saw. I knew it was dangerous, because its aura was crazy red and yellow, especially around its head. I could see it, just waiting for a child to get close, but none of the other children saw it. They acted like nothing was there. "Right there," I shouted with frustration as I pointed. "Just past the base! Can't you see it?"

"Goldeneyes, Goldeneyes, always telling stupid lies!" Bo chanted, swaggering towards third base.

I gripped my smooth stone with the lovely grain, reared back, and threw it as hard as I could at the bad man.

The stone bounced off its head and it cried out. It became less gray, and I guess now the other children could see it because they screamed and began running towards the log schoolhouse.

The creature ignored them. Instead, it charged at me. I shrieked and turned to run, but the bad man was too fast. It knocked me to the ground, grabbed my arm, and bit it.

It froze.

It sniffed.

Then it dropped my arm and stepped back, glaring at me with pale yellow eyes. "Young female!" it snarled, and ran away towards the low shrubs in the gully wash.

Mrs. Graham arrived carrying a long spear with a ragged metal point. She looked around carefully before kneeling beside me.

"He bit me!" I cried. Bright blood flowed from between my fingers as I gripped my arm.

"Is that all it did?" Mrs. Graham checked me over carefully for other injuries. "It only bit your arm?"

"Yes," I said, trying to be brave and not wail. "I'm bleeding!"

"That will help get the poison out." She picked me up and carried me to the log schoolhouse where she had me sit outside the door on a stump. She washed the series of little cuts where its teeth had penetrated, and wrapped my arm with some leaves and tied them on with twine.

"We couldn't see it," said Bo, holding the teacher's spear and looking around the schoolyard. "How come she could?"

"Goldeneyes is a bit special." She wiped her brow and looked into my eyes. "Did you see which way it went after it bit you?"

"Back that way." I sniffed and pointed. "Towards the wash."

Bo touched the point of the spear. "Can we go back and play kickball now?"

I always thought he was a little stupid as well as mean.

Mrs. Graham shook her head. "No, you can't. We need to make a sweep through the wash. We can't let any of the Blur make a den around here."

The children grumbled, and Bo led them into the schoolhouse. There would be no more outside games today.

I nervously kicked the stump with the back of my heels and picked at the leafy bandage. Mrs. Graham sat on the ground and looked at me. "Jia, how did you know the Blur was there?"

"Is that what the bad man was? A Blur?"

"Yes. How did you know it was there?"

"I could see him. It. By third base. He was all gray."

"Why did he attack you?"

I shrugged. "I bounced a rock off his head."

Mrs. Graham started to laugh and then caught herself. "And then he attacked you?"

"Yes." A tear trickled down my cheek. I wanted my mother, not a bunch of questions.

"Why did he run away?"

"Don't know."

The teacher looked at me like grownups do when they don't quite believe what you said but don't know what else to ask. Then she helped me down from the stump. "How does your arm feel?"

"Sore."

"Any stinging? Burning?"

"No."

"Are you sure?"

"Yes."

Then my father came running, and I burst into tears and cried into his chest as he held me. Mrs. Graham explained what had happened, and they agreed everyone needed to get spears and a couple of the precious guns and do a sweep of the wash.

"I don't understand," she said. "She got bit by a full-grown Blur, and yet her arm isn't burning. There was venom in the bite; I could see it where she was bleeding. She ought to be..."

"That's enough," said my father. "Let me take her home." He lifted me up so my head rested against his neck, and started down the path that led to our log cabin.

Over his shoulder, I could see Mrs. Graham, looking puzzled, and the faces of the children sticking out the windows of the schoolhouse. Everyone stared at me. They weren't chanting, but they didn't have to. The echoes were still in my head. "Can't spell, can't read, no one likes a half-breed."

I didn't tell Mrs. Graham or my Dad that I had understood what the bad man had said, that I had understood the Blur. I wasn't supposed to be able to understand them, nobody could, and I guess I wasn't supposed to be able to see them when they were standing still and gone invisible, because nobody could.

But I could and I did.

I really was a half-breed, and everyone knew it.

Half Blur.

Proof

Made in the USA
Charleston, SC
05 May 2012